"What the hell is it about you?" Sax murmured

Without giving Maddy time to answer, his mouth hungrily settled on hers. Heat flared instantly. The shared kiss was unabashedly erotic—hot, openmouthed and ravenous.

Not taking his mouth from hers, he leaned back on the desk and hauled her against him. Maddy went willingly. Eagerly.

"Do you know how close I am to taking you right now?" he growled. "Right here on this desk?" His teeth nipped at the tender skin of her lobe.

"Sax, we can't." Her weak protest was lost as he began to work his erotic magic again.

"Lady, you taste so good." He continued to stroke her everywhere, while he tantalized her mouth and neck with his tongue, igniting embers deep inside her. "You taste like rich warm honey. And sex. And temptation...."

A temptation he had to resist.

JoAnn Ross has written over twenty wonderful Temptation novels, yet each and every one is close to her heart. *Lovestorm* is no exception. "Sax is a strong hero, a cop who'd saved countless people," says JoAnn. "In my story, he's given up on life, till he's healed by the most powerful force—love." JoAnn wishes all her fans a happy holiday. In the New Year, look for #482 *Angel of Desire*, an unusual story about—what else?—an angel!

Books by JoAnn Ross

HARLEQUIN TEMPTATION
382—DARK DESIRES
409—THE KNIGHT IN SHINING ARMOR
432—STAR-CROSSED LOVERS
436—MOONSTRUCK LOVERS
453—THE PRINCE & THE SHOWGIRL

LOVESTORM

JoANN ROSS

Harlequin Books

TORONTO • NEW YORK • LONDON
AMSTERDAM • PARIS • SYDNEY • HAMBURG
STOCKHOLM • ATHENS • TOKYO • MILAN
MADRID • WARSAW • BUDAPEST • AUCKLAND

ISBN 0-373-25571-3

LOVESTORM

Copyright © 1993 by JoAnn Ross.

Printed in U.S.A.

1

THEY WERE GOING to kill her.

The thought flashed through Madeline Delaney's mind, as vivid and deadly as the lightning forking across the storm black sky.

The boat rocked on the churning waves that were cresting at fifteen feet; at the best of times she was not a good sailor, but at the moment Madeline was too frightened to be seasick.

Refusing to give her captors the satisfaction of watching her succumb to the hysteria that was bubbling up inside her, she took a deep breath, focused her whirling mind on some distant, faraway point and struggled for calm.

She took faint comfort from the fact that two of the three men had elected to remain below deck, so there was only a single gun pointed her way. Unfortunately it was a very large gun.

A clap of thunder directly overhead rocked the boat; a flash of lightning illuminated the pitching sea, the jagged, ghostly pillars of sea stacks and the faint shadow of distant land. Having been held under guard below deck, she had no idea of how far away the boat was from the shore.

"You'll never get away with it, you know." She had to shout to be heard over the howling wind.

Her would-be assassin shrugged his massive shoulders and gave her a cold, dangerous smile as he cocked the pistol.

Another clap of thunder boomed. The boat rose and fell, plummeting down the back of a huge swell. Spray hit against the sides of the cabin with the sound of flying gravel.

Suddenly, without warning, there was a thunderous roar as a giant whale breached amid a self-made storm of spray, rising from the water, lunging for the sky.

For that suspended moment, the two humans on the deck froze, stunned by the unexpected sight of twenty tons hovering over them. When the enormous mammal made a thunderous reunion with the sea, a wave washed over the boat's railing. The craft tilted precariously and the man struggled, legs braced, trying to keep from sliding off the slanting, wet deck into the roiling sea.

Realizing that she'd just been given a fleeting stay of execution and knowing that she hadn't exactly been handed a plethora of choices, Madeline closed her eyes and dived headfirst into the whitecapped maelstrom.

A bright streak of light flashed across her peripheral vision. Before her kidnapper could get off a second shot, the churning black tide swallowed her up, covering her like a shroud.

And then she began to swim. For her life.

THE LIGHTHOUSE WAS located on an isolated rock jetty armored with thirty-ton stones and topped with a fringe of wind-bent cypress and shaggy, dark fir trees.

Once it had served to warn ships away from the rocky shoreline; now that duty had been passed on to an automated lighthouse a mile up the windswept northern Oregon coast.

Although Saxon Carstairs regretted the passing of the old seacoast tradition, the first time he'd seen the towering old building that was to become his home—rising through the icy gray fog, isolated from civilization—he was grateful for the coast guard's modernization program.

He'd been living in the lighthouse for nearly a year. And with the exception of the two trips he'd been forced to make to Portland on business, or the once-a-month excursions into Satan's Cove for supplies, he'd remained insistently reclusive.

The remote bit of land was one of the most dangerous locations on the vast Pacific coastline. When the mainland town had been founded over a hundred years ago, its discoverer, Captain Elijah Spalding Gray, had named it Gray's Harbor.

Eventually, as more and more ships foundered in the turbulent waters, the crescent strip of rocky beach became known to all the locals and sea captains—who believed the waters offshore to be cursed—as Satan's Cove.

Then, eighty years ago, in a bit of serendipity, a misinformed cartographer for Rand McNally had inadvertently and literally put the town's nickname, rather than its actual name of Gray's Harbor, on the map. The name stuck.

The jetty on which the lighthouse was located was more than three miles long, which would have kept all but the most intrepid coastal hiker from paying him a visit.

But even that unlikely possibility had been short-circuited by an October typhoon that had washed away part of the stone jetty, effectively turning it into an island. Which was just the way Sax liked it.

Because he'd had his fill of civilization.

There had been a time, in what now seemed like another lifetime, when he'd been filled with an overwhelming need to not only participate in society, but to make it better.

Unfortunately justice had proven to be not only blindfolded, but deaf and dumb, as well, and Sax had learned the hard way that one man couldn't save the world from itself.

Unable to save the world, he'd chosen to retreat from it entirely. Now all he wanted was a chance to build himself a quiet, uneventful life where he didn't have to worry about some coked-up drug dealer pumping bullets into him.

Sax stood outside on the observation deck that surrounded the top floor of the lighthouse, high above the sea, heedless of the wind whipping at his clothes as he watched the late-afternoon squall develop into a violent storm.

Although it was not yet time for the sun to set, the sky had turned a dark pewter color. Black-edged clouds rumbled across the metallic gray sky; periodic bursts of lightning bathed the landscape in stuttering flashes of sulfurous light.

Gazing through the telephoto lens of his camera, Sax saw geysers of water, monumental clouds of spray and foamlike explosions several hundred yards offshore. He clicked away, catching the wondrous sight of the migratory whales breaching.

A pod of the gigantic mammals were leaping into the air and crashing back into the sea. They were quite literally playing with the storm. The same wind capable of capsizing a ship was currently providing a boisterous playground for the whales.

Several of them began sailing, tails held aloft above the surface at right angles to the fifty-knot wind approaching the shore. Then just when he felt certain they'd beach themselves on the treacherous rocks, they'd turn around, heading back out to sea for another sail.

They were mostly California grays, on their annual six-thousand-mile migratory spring trek up the Pacific Coast from their mating and birthing grounds off the Baja coast back to the Bering Sea.

He sharpened the lens's focus, catching sight of a few humpback whales, along with the more familiar dolphins. Although they were relatively rare in these waters, locals had informed him that a few pods of humpback whales were spotted every season.

Although he'd prefer just to stand at the railing and enjoy the sight, Sax realized that what he was viewing was not only impressive, but it was also highly marketable. Since his police pension was nothing to shout about, Sax turned his mind to work.

He could think of at least three magazines that would pay for photographs of whales breaching. Not to mention all those tourists who flocked to the coastal towns every summer.

Last season several small galleries from Gold Beach to Astoria had quickly sold out their stock of his photographs. That success had led to interest from Portland collectors, which had necessitated the unwelcome trips into the city.

Fortunately Sax had an agent to handle all his business dealings. He knew that if it were up to him to glad-hand all those gallery owners, babbling on about aesthetics versus craft and negotiating percentages over glasses of trendy white wine, he'd still be waiting to sell his first photograph.

He'd gone through five rolls of film when he caught sight of the boat bobbing dangerously between the horizon and the coast.

"Damn idiot." Any fisherman or recreational sailor stupid enough to go out on a day like this deserved whatever punishment the fates dished out.

Focusing the lens on the wildly pitching boat, Sax could make out two figures on deck. Deciding that there was no end to human stupidity, he snapped the shutter release, thinking the photo might prove an interesting study of human frailty—or idiocy. Then he turned back to the boisterous pod of whales and continued clicking away.

But his heart was no longer in his work.

Cursing darkly, he went into the lighthouse and, although the enormous prism lens that had once warned sailors away from the rocky coast was no longer operational, he turned on all the lights on both the second and third floors.

It began to rain; water pelted against the thick window glass like bullets. Sax wasn't certain whether the incandescent lamps could be seen through the heavy rain, but he'd done all he could.

If the boat ended up foundering or crashing up on the rocky shore, there would be nothing he could do to help whatever fools were on board.

Besides, they weren't his responsibility, he reminded himself. Dammit, he'd earned the right not to care.

SHE WAS NOT DEAD. Not yet. Unfortunately the water was even icier than it had looked. Swimming was proving impossible. The storm-tossed sea had her in its grip, tumbling her as a child would play with a brightly colored beach ball.

Madeline's arms and legs felt as if they were frozen, and worse yet, with pelting rain obscuring the jagged coastline, Madeline couldn't tell whether she was headed toward the relative safety of the shore or being dragged fatally out to sea.

She caught sight of a fin moving through the water and bit back a scream, trying to remember if there were sharks in these waters. If there were, her frantic attempts to swim would be bound to garner their attention. Scenes from *Jaws* flashed through her turmoiled mind, terrifying in their reality.

And then she saw it. A faint, welcoming light in the distance. The dim glow seemed impossibly far away.

There was a blinding pain at the back of her head; her lungs were burning. Her icy limbs felt like lead weights; it was all she could do to keep them moving. A wave crested over her head, and for a long, terrifying time she couldn't breathe.

Finally, just when she thought she would surely drown, Madeline popped to the surface again. Gasping for breath in an attempt to fill her starving lungs, she swallowed another mouthful of salt water.

Another wave swept over her. *It's no use*, Madeline thought bleakly as she felt herself being dragged even deeper into the blackness by a vicious undertow. She'd done her best to escape, but in the end, all that she'd accomplished was doing her assailants' dirty work for them.

Her lungs felt as if they were going to explode. Above the roiling surf, the storm continued to rage. Beneath the surface, in the cold, dark belly of the ocean, the silence was monumental.

Suddenly she heard a chorus of sounds—eerie *wheeeps* and low, rumbling sighs—that boomed and echoed and swelled. The song was so intense she could feel it, like drums beating inside her head, throbbing through her body.

Blinking against the sting of the salt water in her eyes, she saw the mighty whale's approach. Although she knew it must be her imagination, stimulated by lack of oxygen, she felt the mammal was attempting, with its sorrowful song and doleful gaze, to be offering some sort of reassurance. At the last minute, displaying magnificent grace for such an enormous animal, it artfully lifted its flipper to avoid contact with her.

At the same time, from behind the mighty whale, a dolphin approached, talking in a coda of staccato clicks and whistles. The creature touched her in a remarkably gentle fashion with its slim gray snout, then dived beneath her, amazingly nudging her upward until her head broke the surface of the water.

Madeline had heard stories of these gregarious mammals assisting drowning sailors but had never believed them. Neither could she quite believe it now.

Certain that she must be hallucinating but unwilling to turn her back on what might actually be her only chance of survival, Madeline managed to grasp hold of the dolphin's dorsal fin.

Closing her eyes, she hung on with every last vestige of her strength, sailing shoreward on a sea of unearthly music.

THIS WAS RIDICULOUS. Sax cursed and poured himself a drink. The storm was raging with nearly the strength of last autumn's typhoon. The wind was blowing at gale force, the waves were washing over the rocky precipice, and the rain had become a deluge.

Not that he need worry. The lights were still on, he had a backup generator in the event power did go out, the hundred-year-old lighthouse had been built to weather worse storms than this, so he was safe, dry and comfortable.

Unlike those empty-headed idiots on that damn boat. The very same boat that had now disappeared somewhere between the rocky shore and the horizon.

There was nothing he could do, Sax told himself over and over again. Nothing.

As he took a long swallow of the Scotch, he envisioned the small craft washing up onto the rocks of his jetty. He pictured the occupants, broken and bleeding, their lungs filled with salt water, needing someone, anyone, to save their lives.

Muttering a string of virulent curses, he tossed back the rest of the liquor, slammed the glass down onto the table and went downstairs to retrieve his foul-weather gear.

The wail of the wind echoed like a lost spirit, reminding Sax of all the sea captains who'd lost both their ships and their lives along this same rocky shore.

When he'd first arrived on the coast, Wilma Nelson, the proprietor of the Gray Whale Mercantile, Satan's Cove's general store, had informed him that his lighthouse was haunted by all the souls of the men who'd perished in these icy waters.

Being burdened with ghosts of his own, Sax hadn't been disturbed by the elderly woman's assertion. What were a few more lost souls? More or less?

The pelting rain stung his face. Hunching his shoulders, he made his way along the rocky shoreline, stepping over the new supply of driftwood and kelp that had washed ashore.

He looked out to sea, but he still couldn't see the boat. So intent was he on catching sight of it that he nearly tripped over her.

She was lying facedown in a tidal pool. Her soaked jeans, lightweight red cotton sweater and sneakers were hardly appropriate attire for a stormy day at sea. Her hair flowed out behind her; it was too filthy and tangled with seaweed to determine its color, but he suspected that it would be an ordinary shade of brown. When he turned her over, her complexion was a sickly gray he'd seen before.

Fool. He squatted down beside her and pressed his thumb and middle finger on either side of her trachea.

"Breathe, dammit," he growled when he failed to find a pulse.

Since there was no indication of neck injury, he tilted her head backward to open the airway. Pinching her nostrils closed, he placed his mouth tightly over hers, then exhaled quickly and deeply, four times in rapid succession, each time removing his mouth and letting the air escape passively from between her lips. Another breath followed.

He dragged her from the water without interrupting his artificial respiration. As soon as he had her on the wet gray sand, he placed the heel of his left hand on her sternum, put the heel of his right atop the left and began administering CPR.

Breathe, compress, breathe, compress, two ventilations interposed between every fifteen compressions. Sax could have done the lifesaving cardiopulmonary resuscitation technique in his sleep.

Although later, when she remembered this moment, she would be certain that she must have imagined it, Madeline felt as if she were rising free of her painful, aching body, hovering over the man and the woman on the beach.

The man was alternately pounding on her chest and breathing into her mouth. The woman—why, it was her! Madeline realized with a numb, disconnected awareness—was lying on the wet sand, deathly still.

She wanted to tell him to stop. That it wasn't any use, that they'd won, after all. But then she realized that she had no memory of who had done this to her. On top of that came the understanding that it was very important that she find out.

Reluctantly, as soft and silent as breath, she slipped back into the supine female body.

Finally she began to breathe. At first raggedly, then to his vast relief, her respiration grew stronger. Sax held her as she began to cough up the seawater she'd swallowed. Her retching seemed to come from her very depths.

With a sudden display of strength that took him by surprise, she flailed at him, desperately striking out with the ferocity of a cornered wildcat. She was clawing at his face, going for his eyes, trying to scratch them out with her broken fingernails.

"Hey! It's okay," Sax shouted.

Her brain had shut down. Her body, which had been limp and lifeless only moments earlier, bucked frantically in an attempt to escape. She was acting instinctively, kicking and writhing, struggling desperately to save herself.

Sax swore swiftly and violently as her nails raked down the side of his face. Frustrated, he caught both her hands, moving deftly aside when she tried to knee him in the groin.

"Dammit, lady, I'm not going to hurt you."

He held her captured hands in one of his and began stroking her wet and tangled hair away from her too-pale face with the other. Although he had never thought of himself as a gentle man, his tone and his touch sought to reassure.

"You're on shore," he soothed gruffly. "You're not in any danger anymore. You're safe." He ran his fingers down her cheek and over her icy white lips. "Safe," he repeated.

Her eyes lost a bit of their wild fear as they desperately searched his face. Her lashes were unattractively clumped together from salt water and tears. Sax watched as she made her decision.

"Thank you," she managed on something between a gasp and a whisper.

Then her lids fluttered closed again.

But her breathing remained steady. Frail and stuttering, but steady, Sax determined. Scooping her into his arms, he flung her over his shoulder and began walking back over the moss-covered rocks toward the lighthouse.

He was not surprised to discover that he'd locked the door behind him. Old habits—like locking doors and rescuing maidens in distress—Sax decided as he dug into his pockets for the key ring, obviously died hard.

Although her clothes were soaking, she wasn't at all heavy. There had been a time when he could have carried double her weight twice the distance and not even been winded. Now, thanks to his long, solitary runs along the beach, his stamina had returned. In fact, he was stronger and fitter than he'd been before what he could only refer to as "the incident."

The near-fatal shooting had taken his partner's life and given Sax a firsthand glimpse of the lowest circles of hell. It had also left him with scars—both physical and mental—that he knew he'd carry for the rest of his life.

He considered putting her on the downstairs couch, but decided that she'd be more comfortable in his bed. Carrying her upstairs, he laid her on the mattress and quickly and efficiently dispensed with her soaked sneakers and stripped her wet jeans off, frowning at the bruises on her hips, thighs and calves.

She'd hurt like the devil in the morning. But at least she'd know she was alive.

The flesh that wasn't black-and-blue was lightly tanned to the color of honey, indicating that she must not be a local. In the eleven months he'd been living on the coast, the skies had dumped more than one hundred inches of rain on the jetty, giving credence to the old axiom that Oregonians never tanned—they rusted.

He pulled the sodden sweater over her head and tossed it onto the floor. Her hair got tangled on a button for a brief moment, and when he took his hand away, Sax frowned at the blood darkening the tips of his fingers. Brushing her wet hair out of the way, he examined the wound.

He wouldn't have been all that surprised to see a deep gash from the treacherous rocks that lined the shore of the jetty. But this cut was not caused by any rock. He'd been a cop long enough to recognize a graze from a bullet when he saw one.

Sax frowned and lifted his gaze to the window, looking out toward the blackened sea. Whoever had been on that boat with her had obviously tried to kill her. But why?

It didn't matter, dammit. It was a problem for the authorities, not him. It wasn't any of his damn business.

In fact, his first instinct was to put the woman's clothes back on and take her to the beach where he'd found her and wash his hands of her and whatever problem she'd gotten herself into.

But he knew he couldn't do it. Because he'd been fool enough to strap on his damn tarnished armor and go riding off to rescue a fair maiden yet again, he was stuck with her. At least until the weather cleared enough to get her to the mainland.

The sky had turned as black as the sea; there was no point in searching for her assailants. And he couldn't call the coast guard because he'd resisted having a phone installed in the lighthouse.

Sax let out a long, frustrated sigh as he looked down at the woman he'd literally dragged from the sea. She certainly didn't look like some gorgeous mythical mermaid. She was wet and sandy and too thin for his taste.

She also looked horribly frail and vulnerable lying on his wide bed, seaweed tangled in her hair, her slender body covered with bruises and scrapes. There was another bad scrape on her face, along the slanted line of her cheekbone.

He retrieved a towel and a brown bottle of hydrogen peroxide from the bathroom. When he began to clean the wound, her eyes flew open.

"It's okay," he said quickly in an attempt to avoid her having another panic attack. "I'm just cleaning you up a little. See?" He held up the wet corner of the towel as evidence of his honorable intent.

It was obvious that she was trying to talk but found the effort too much. Her eyes were the color of aged whiskey and laced with pain as they pleaded eloquently with him.

"Don't worry," Sax said gruffly, hating the way her mute defenselessness moved something unwelcome deep inside him. "I won't let them hurt you."

Once again her gaze moved slowly over his face, searching, assessing. Once again she decided to trust. Once again she slipped into unconsciousness.

Sax finished cleaning the wound, then sat on the edge of the bed, looking down at her.

Her underwear was lacking any lace or frilly feminine adornment. Instead of a bra, she was wearing a

sleeveless ribbed white cotton undershirt, much like
Sax remembered his father wearing.

Although on her it looked a great deal different. The
wet cotton clung to her body like a second skin; her
nipples, pebbled by the cold, thrust erotically against
the fabric. The bikini panties, cut high on the thigh,
were the same color and fabric as the shirt.

Until this moment, if he'd been asked, Sax would
have said that his preference in female lingerie would
have been frothy silk-and-satin confections. But that
was before he'd seen what this woman could do to an
undershirt and cotton panties.

As he felt a slow, deep pull of desire, Sax swore and
dragged his hand over his face. What the hell was the
matter with him? What kind of man had he become, to
react so physically to an unconscious woman?

A man who'd been without female companionship
too long, Sax decided. After all, he'd been flat on his
back in the hospital for six months. After his release,
he'd spent the past eleven months locked away here in
his lighthouse.

The idea that it was nothing more than nearly a year
and a half of self-enforced celibacy that had his body
hardening at the dark shadow between her slender
thighs proved vastly comforting.

Returning his mind to the matters at hand, Sax took
a deep breath and stripped off the woman's wet, in-
nocently seductive underwear, intending to wash it
with the rest of her clothing.

The bedspread was now sprinkled with wet, dark
gray sand; a few grains continued to cling to her skin.
Deciding that there was no point in challenging temptation any further than he already had, he elected not

to brush them away. In the morning he'd let her take a
bath.

He pulled one of his old T-shirts over her head, then
managed to drag the bedspread from beneath her limp
body and tuck her between the navy blue sheets. When
she failed to open her eyes, he checked her pulse again,
pleased to find it a great deal stronger. From her slow,
steady breathing, he determined that she was no longer
unconscious, merely sleeping.

"Sweet dreams," he murmured, giving in to temptation just long enough to run the back of his hand
down the unbruised side of her face. "It appears you've
earned them."

Gathering up the discarded clothing from the floor,
he went back downstairs to the kitchen, where he put
them in the washing machine, adding an extra scoop
of detergent for good measure.

After checking to make certain the door was se-
curely bolted—although he doubted that her attackers
had survived the storm, he wasn't about to take any
chances—he went back upstairs, pulled a chair up beside the bed and sat vigil.

"Who the hell are you?" he asked. "And who wanted
you dead badly enough to risk going out in that storm?"

When she didn't wake to answer his muttered query,
Sax was left pondering the possibilities.

Hours later, he'd just nodded off when he'd heard her
crying, a soft, whimpering weeping that captured his
immediate attention. That, along with her shivering,
created an unwilling surge of masculine protective instinct.

Sighing, he pulled back the blankets and joined her in the wide bed, drawing her against him, sharing his warmth.

"It's okay," he repeated what he'd told her earlier, on the beach. "Nobody's going to hurt you."

But whatever had transpired on that boat had obviously frightened her badly. Although she stopped trembling and the weeping gradually ceased, he couldn't keep her still.

She kept muttering incoherently in her sleep, tossing and turning like those storm-tossed waves she'd been cast adrift in.

He tried to keep her covered, but every time he pulled the sheet and blanket over her, she'd scissor her legs, frantically kicking them off, as if she was dreaming of her dangerous swim.

When she suddenly sat bolt upright and tried to leap out of bed, Sax grabbed her, pulling her down on top of him.

She wiggled fiercely, with a strength that once again surprised him, but he steadfastly refused to let go. Instead, he anchored her to him with one strong arm while stroking her hair, her back, with his free hand. All the time he kept murmuring words of reassurance over and over.

Eventually her frantic struggles ceased. Exhausted, she collapsed on top of him, gave a soft sigh of submission and drifted back to sleep.

The T-shirt was twisted around her waist. Her soft breasts were pressed against his chest, her pelvis was right on top of his jeans placket, and her bare legs were draped indecorously across his thighs.

He'd definitely been too long without a woman, Sax decided as he felt his body hardening instinctively to the feel of a woman pressed so seductively against it.

Even as he told himself that he had absolutely no desire to get involved in any type of *relationship*—now there was a female word if he'd ever heard one—from his reaction to this woman, it was obvious that his body and his mind were not in agreement.

Once he turned his uninvited guest over to the local authorities, he was going to go straight to Davey Jones's Locker—a local tavern catering to fishermen. Iris, the redheaded barmaid with the Miss Universe body, had been throwing increasingly overt sexual invitations his way ever since his arrival in Satan's Cove.

His scowl and his brusque manner had effectively discouraged the one hundred and thirty-five citizens of Satan's Cove from engaging him in casual conversation. After a few attempts to welcome him to their close-knit community, most individuals had gotten the idea and were content to leave him alone. Everyone, that is, except Iris.

The thirty-something woman was as openly friendly as a puppy, and appeared to honestly like everyone she'd ever met. She'd invited Sax home with her the first night he'd shown up at the bar and proceeded to get slowly and deliberately drunk.

Later, when he looked back on that night, he would be embarrassed at how blunt his refusal had been, but Iris, never one to hold a grudge, had proven to possess the tenacity of an aluminum-siding salesman.

Eleven months later she was still telling him, in both words and actions, that he was always welcome in her home—and in her bed.

And then, of course, there was Ellen. The last time he'd been in Portland, his ex-wife had made it clear that although she did not want to be Mrs. Saxon Carstairs, she wouldn't mind sleeping with him again. For old times' sake.

Although his relationship with Ellen had become remarkably amiable, in contrast to their two-year marriage, which had proven a war zone, Sax would rather take a midnight swim stark naked with a bunch of sharks than make the mistake of getting emotionally involved with his beautiful ex-wife again.

The woman's breath was like a soft summer breeze against his throat. As the sharp claws of desire dug a little deeper, Sax decided that it was probably time he took the extremely beddable Iris up on her offer.

Oblivious to his lustful male thoughts, the sleeping woman squirmed again, fitting her body even closer to his.

Sax groaned.

It was definitely going to be a long night.

2

IT WAS THE SOUND of the wind, moaning like a lost spirit, and the rain, pelting like stones against the window, that woke her.

Disoriented, Madeline struggled to sit up, wishing she hadn't done so when the gingerly executed movement caused rocks to begin tumbling around in her head. She dragged her hand through her tangled hair, cringing as her fingers got caught in the strands of dried kelp.

Her entire body ached. Tentatively she lifted the navy blue sheet away and saw why. The flesh not covered by the unfamiliar T-shirt was darkened with purple bruises and angry red scrapes. She was still trying to figure out exactly how that could have happened when the fact that she'd awakened nearly nude in a strange bed sank in.

She glanced around the unfamiliar room with a gnawing sense of doom. Her eyes stung; she blinked several times in an attempt to moisten them, but her lids felt as if they were scraping against gravel.

The strange bed she'd awakened in appeared to have been carved in a four-poster Shaker style; its clean, simple lines matched the plain, whitewashed walls adorned with framed photographs of stormy seascapes.

She managed, with no small effort, to climb out of the bed. Wincing at the pain in her bruised hips, she hobbled across the octagonal room to the window and looked out.

Through the thick bank of fog, she could see that a storm was raging. From time to time, the wind would part the thick gray curtain of fog, allowing her to catch a glimpse of a turbulent sea.

Although the landscape was every bit as unfamiliar as this room, when she viewed the angry whitecapped waves, Madeline felt an icy frisson of fear race up her spine. Gooseflesh rose on her bare arms, and she began to tremble.

Rubbing her arms, she turned away from the window. There was something frightening out there. Something she'd have to face. Later. After she understood what was happening to her. And why.

It occurred to her that perhaps the answer was in this room. She returned to the bed and had just pulled open the drawer of the pine bedside table when she heard the unmistakable sound of a footfall on the stairs outside the closed door.

Terror lodged in her throat. Her panic-stricken eyes swept the room, looking for some way to escape.

And then she saw the gun. As she took the wicked-looking revolver from the drawer, the metal felt cold and deadly. Drawing in a deep breath, she gripped the weapon tightly with both hands, aimed it directly at the door and waited.

SAX WASN'T SURPRISED when he failed to discover any sign of the missing craft. It was, after all, an enormous ocean and a long coastline; even if the boat had capsized, the odds of any pieces of it washing up on his jetty would have been slight.

His morning search of the rocks had also confirmed something else he'd suspected. The normally rough channel between his jetty and the coast was too dangerous to risk taking the woman to the mainland on the launch.

For the first time since his arrival on the coast, he wondered if he should have given in to Ellen's urging that he at least put a two-way radio in the lighthouse.

But dammit, in the eleven months he'd been living in the lighthouse, he hadn't had any use for either a telephone or a radio. Until now.

So it looked as if he was stuck with the damn woman. At least for the time being. He jammed his fists into the pockets of his jacket and glared out at the still-raging sea, as if he could make the waters lower with the sheer strength of his not inconsiderable will. The sooner they receded, the better.

He couldn't wait to put his uninvited visitor into the launch and hand her over to the authorities on the mainland. Then he'd be off the hook.

Returning to the lighthouse, he heard a movement upstairs, evidence that the woman was awake. After retrieving her laundered clothing from the dryer, he climbed the circular staircase to the second floor.

Sax knocked once.

Twice.

Failing to receive an answer, he opened the door and found himself facing the business end of his service revolver.

"Come one step closer and I'll shoot," she warned.

Lord, he'd thought the woman had looked bad last night. This morning, in the cold gray light of day, she appeared even more pitiful.

Her bare arms and legs were covered with scrapes and bruises, her face was still as pale as a wraith, and her tangled, filthy hair, falling over her shoulders, reminded him of one of Macbeth's witches.

Her wide eyes resembled those of a trapped animal. But along with the fear, he saw a feverish determination glowing in their whiskey brown depths, telling him that she would actually pull the trigger, if pushed.

However, from the way her hands were trembling, he doubted if she were capable of even hitting the side of his lighthouse, let alone a man standing across the room.

"I'm not going to hurt you." His voice was low and calm. "I was just bringing you your clothes. See?" He showed her the folded clothing. "All clean."

She didn't take her gaze from his face. "Get down on the floor. On your knees."

"Oh, for the love of—"

"On the floor!" Her voice held a high-pitched staccato sound Sax had heard before. It was the tone of a person about to lose control. That was all he needed— a hysterical female with a gun in her hands. Her knuckles whitened as she gripped the revolver tighter. "And put your hands behind your head."

Cursing, he dropped her clothes, then knelt on the plank floor, linking his fingers together at the back of his neck.

"In case you've forgotten, I'm the one who pulled you out of the drink last night," he said mildly.

She glared at him with wary but defiant eyes. Her slender body remained as rigid as cold steel. "The drink?"

"The ocean. I found you in a tidal pool, gave you CPR, brought you back here, cleaned your wound and put you to bed. I'm also the man you drove crazy all night."

He saw something that looked like memory stir in her brown eyes.

An image was teasing at the far reaches of Madeline's mind. A hazy mental picture of herself lying on the beach with a large man kneeling over her, stubbornly breathing life into her lungs.

This man, she realized, possessed the same ebony hair as the man in her vision. It framed the hard planes of his face in a shaggy, careless style that reminded her vaguely of swashbuckling pirates. Or old-time Western outlaws.

His hooded eyes were a dark slate; his nose was bluntly carved and looked as if it had been broken at one time. The imperfection, she decided, went well with his angular, aggressive jawline. His mouth was a harsh, unsmiling slash bracketed by grim lines of experience. Those rugged lines, along with the sprinkling of silver at his temples, made her guess his age to be somewhere in his late thirties.

There was a hardness about the man, a rough, unsparing toughness that set her nerves even more on edge. Her fingers tightened almost imperceptibly on the gun as a knot of uncertainty coiled tightly in her stomach. "You saved my life?"

He shrugged. "I didn't have a hell of a lot of choices. Seeing how you washed up on my shore."

"I was drowning." The suddenly vivid memory of being dragged beneath the icy, dark waters caused her to start trembling again.

"That'd be my guess," Sax agreed. His gaze swept over her, revealing no curiosity, friendliness, irritation. No nothing. "You'd also been shot."

"Shot?" She glanced down uncomprehendingly at the revolver in her hand. "With a gun?"

"That's right."

She swallowed. "Not this gun?"

"Hell, no."

Somehow she hadn't thought so. "If I was shot, why am I still alive?"

"You were lucky. It was only a graze. At the back of your head," he elaborated at her sharp, questioning look. "Behind your right ear."

She tentatively lifted her hand to the spot, cringing slightly when her fingertips brushed against the tender raw skin. "Who would want to shoot me?"

"You could probably answer that question a lot better than I could," Sax suggested. "Since I don't even know your name."

"Madeline."

"That's a start. Madeline who?"

Her complexion turned even paler, if that was possible. Confused brown eyes darkened; she shook her head dazedly. "I don't know."

Sax studied her intently. "Let me get this straight. You're saying you don't know your last name?"

"No." It was only a whisper, but easily heard in the sudden stillness of the bedroom.

He watched her absorb the implications of her situation. That she was honestly distressed was all too obvious. Determined to keep his emotional distance, Sax shook off the unwilling feeling of sympathy.

"Does that mean you've no idea what you were doing out on that boat in the middle of a storm, or who it was who tried to kill you? Or why?"

She tried to talk, but the words wouldn't come.

"Take your time," Sax advised.

She swallowed, then tried again. "No." She began to sway on her feet. "Oh, God," she moaned, dragging her trembling fingers through her hair. "I'm in trouble, aren't I?"

"It's probably just the result of trauma," he said musingly. "It's not uncommon to experience some short-term retrograde amnesia after a head injury."

"Are you a doctor?"

"No, but I've seen it happen."

"Oh?" She bit her lip and looked at him uneasily.

The sight of her teeth worrying the soft pink flesh of her lower lip created a distant stir. One Sax refused to acknowledge. "I used to be a cop. One of the good guys," he added significantly. When her expression turned decidedly skeptical, he said, "Hey, it's easy enough to check out."

She glanced around the room. "You're right. The thing to do is to call the authorities and confirm your identity."

Sax noted that the woman certainly had no trouble making a quick decision in spite of her injury and stress. He found that mildly interesting even as he vowed to remain uninvolved.

"There's a slight problem with that idea. I don't have a phone." His unsatisfactory answer caused her to look at him with renewed suspicion. "But my old shield is in the same drawer you got that gun from," he said. "My name is Saxon Carstairs. My friends call me Sax."

He decided not to point out that since it had been a very long time since he'd engaged in any social activities, he wasn't sure he actually had any friends anymore. There wasn't any point in making her more nervous than she obviously was.

Glancing down into the open drawer, she spied the metal badge, lying beside where the gun had been. Then she studied the gun she'd almost forgotten she was holding. "I suppose that badge explains what you're doing with a Smith & Wesson police revolver," she said.

"Interesting you should recognize the make."

She seemed surprised by his quiet observation. "I did, didn't I?"

"Maybe you're a cop yourself." That would explain a lot, he decided.

She frowned, then shook her head. "I don't think so. If I was a police officer, I'd probably feel a great deal more comfortable holding this, wouldn't I?"

The edgy note of fear had faded; her voice, Sax noted, was pleasantly husky. "Probably. You know, you could always put it down. If you're that uncomfortable."

"Oh. Right." She lowered the revolver slowly and placed it on the tabletop.

"Is it all right if I stand up now?" Sax asked.

Color, the first he'd seen since dragging her from the tide pool, rose in her cheeks, revealing her embarrassment.

"I'm sorry. I didn't mean to threaten you that way, in your own home, and especially after you saved my life, but . . ." Her voice trailed off despairingly, and she looked away from him.

"I understand." He stood up slowly, carefully, not wanting to take the chance of spooking her again. An edgy female—even one without a deadly weapon—was enough to make any man nervous. "After what you've obviously been through, you had every right to want to protect yourself."

"You're probably right," she agreed on a sad little sigh. "Still, you must think I'm paranoid, pointing a gun at you after you saved my life."

He waved his hand in a nonchalant gesture of dismissal. "I've always found that a certain degree of paranoia is an admirable trait. There are times when it helps keep a man, or in your case, a woman," he allowed, tilting his head toward her, "alive."

Reluctantly giving her points for strength—most women would be either hysterical or in tears when faced with such a treacherous situation—Sax picked up the revolver, spun the cylinder and returned it to the drawer. "Besides, it wasn't loaded."

"It wasn't?"

He managed a dry, faint smile. Sax couldn't remember the last time he'd found anything to smile about. The unfamiliar expression made him feel as if his face were cracking. "Didn't anyone ever tell you that it's dangerous to keep a loaded gun around the house?" he asked.

One corner of his harshly cut lips quirked in what Madeline suspected might be a hint of good humor. If so, it would be the first indication of any emotion she'd seen thus far. When the faint smile failed to reach his impenetrable dark eyes, she decided that she must have imagined it.

"Yes. My father always told me that."

"Uh-huh. Now we're getting somewhere. What's your father's name?"

Her brow furrowed. "Dad," she said finally. Her shoulders slumped. "Damn." She shook her head, then cringed at the resultant pain.

Her look of distress made his chest ache. Sax had a sudden urge to put his arms around her. He resisted the ludicrous notion. He was the last man capable of offering comfort to anyone.

"Don't worry," he said instead. "It'll all come back. The trick is not to push. In the meantime, no one's going to hurt you again. The way that boat was pitching around on those waves, it's probably been reduced to kindling by now. Besides, you probably haven't noticed, but you're in a lighthouse. No one can get onto this island until the storm passes."

He watched the tension slowly flow out of her neck, her shoulders, her arms.

"I need a bath," she decided. "It's no wonder I can't think clearly. I must have a ton of sand and seaweed in my hair." She wrinkled her nose. There was a faint sprinkling of freckles on the bridge of that slender nose that he hadn't noticed earlier. "And I smell like wet kelp."

"Why don't you sit down and I'll go fill the tub for you?"

"You needn't bother."

"It's no bother. You should probably stay off your feet as much as possible."

"Oh." She considered that. "I suppose you're right. I do seem to have a horrendous headache." That was an understatement. She felt as if an entire orchestra was playing the anvil chorus inside her skull.

"I've got some pain pills that'll fix that. One of those babies, and you won't feel a thing."

He left the room. When he returned, she was standing by the window, staring out at the fog-draped sea.

"I know this is going to sound like a horrible cliché," she said, turning toward him with a faint, embarrassed smile, "but where am I?"

"Satan's Cove." When that failed to bring any spark of recognition to her eyes, he added, "Oregon."

"Oregon?" She chewed thoughtfully on a fingernail as she turned to look back out at the storm. "What in the world am I doing in Oregon?"

"I don't know. But I'll go downstairs and fix breakfast while you take your bath. Perhaps after you've got some bacon and eggs under your belt, you'll get your strength back."

She was looking out the window again. Her slender shoulders were slumped disconsolately, making her appear suddenly very small and very vulnerable. "And my memory?"

"It's worth a try. Besides, I'm starving. And I hate to eat alone."

She turned back toward him, her solemn brown gaze sweeping his face. "I thought you said that you were one of the good guys."

"I am." He handed her a white tablet and a glass of water. "Here."

She eyed the pain medication with reluctance. "I don't think I normally take pills."

"You probably don't normally get shot, then drown, either," Sax pointed out. "Don't worry, it's not habit forming."

The pill was also the lightest strength of all the drugs the doctors had pumped through his system during six long and painful months of enforced hospitalization. Those first weeks, he'd been so heavily drugged he hadn't felt a thing.

Later he'd discovered the hard way exactly how much pain a man could endure and still survive.

Her wary gaze went from the pain tablet to Sax's face, then back to the pill again. The woman was the most openly expressive person Sax had ever seen; every emotion she was feeling, every thought, was broadcast across her face and in her eyes. That could be a fatally dangerous flaw when someone was out to kill you, he considered.

Once again he felt an unbidden masculine urge to protect this woman. Once again he vowed to resist.

Madeline watched his chiseled face turn hard as granite. His eyes were as gray as the sky outside. And suddenly just as cold. With the faintest shrug of her shoulders, she swallowed the pill, finishing off the water. Her throat was sore from swallowing all that salt water during her escape, but it tasted wonderful.

"You know," she said mildly, "my memory isn't entirely gone. I do seem to recall from television police shows that the good guys aren't supposed to lie."

"I don't." His tone was rough. Gritty.

"Don't you?" She handed the empty glass back to him.

Now there was a definite sparkle in her eyes. Could she actually be teasing him? Sax wondered. After all she'd been through?

"No," he repeated firmly, giving her another one of those cool, inscrutable looks. "I never lie."

She studied him again for a long, silent time, looking hard, looking deep. "Perhaps not about the important things," she decided. "But you said you didn't like eating alone. If that were true, you certainly wouldn't be living in this lighthouse on an inaccessible island off the Oregon coast."

"You may have a point," Sax allowed gruffly.

"I've been told I'm very perceptive," Madeline agreed.

"By whom?"

"By—" She frowned and rubbed her temples wearily with her fingertips. "Good try. But I still can't remember. Damn."

"The trick is to relax," he repeated. He picked up the clean clothes he'd dropped onto the floor and placed them on the bed. "I know it's difficult, Maddy, but you can only push yourself so far."

Her lips curved upward as her frown slowly metamorphosed into a slight smile. "My father calls me Maddy," she murmured.

"There you go," Sax said reassuringly. "See? You're already starting to get your memory back. By the time you have your second cup of coffee, you'll probably remember everything."

Her faint smile faded as she returned her gaze out the window to the storm-tossed sea. "You're probably going to think I'm a terrible coward."

Sax thought about the way she'd fought like a tiger last night when she'd thought he was her assailant; he pictured the determination on her face when she'd been pointing his service revolver at him. He considered the effort it must have taken her to even attempt swimming in that icy sea and decided whoever this woman was, no one would ever be able to call her a coward.

"Fear isn't cowardly," he said. "Someone shot you, Maddy. You'd be crazy not to be afraid. Especially since you can't remember who tried to harm you. Or why."

"That's just it," she insisted.

Her strain showed in her bloodshot eyes, in the lines bracketing her mouth. More lines furrowed her brow; Sax resisted the urge to reach out and rub them away.

"I realize that this is probably going to sound crazy," she continued, "but I have the strangest feeling that what I'm really afraid of is remembering."

He'd seen that happen before. He recalled a woman who'd been held hostage at gunpoint by her husband for a harrowing eight hours before he'd finally shot himself in front of her. Afterward, when she couldn't remember a thing about that terrifying event, the police psychologist had explained that dissociation was not all that uncommon among victims following extreme distress or physical risk.

Add to that the fact that Madeline had suffered a bullet graze to the head, and Sax decided that amnesia was not unexpected.

"Believe me, what you're feeling isn't that unusual," he assured her again.

"If you say so," she murmured distractedly as another thought made its way to the forefront of her mind. "Something just occurred to me. If no one can get onto this island until the storm passes, it follows that no one can get off it, either."

"That's about it," Sax agreed. "So it looks as if we're stuck with each other." His tone was gruff, but Maddy thought she detected an undertone of caring. "But you don't have to worry. Because I won't let anything happen to you."

Madeline folded her arms and observed him with renewed interest and a faint smile. "Am I in protective custody?"

"It'd be a little difficult to put you in custody, since I'm not a cop any longer," he reminded her. His closed expression told her that topic was off limits.

"How long were you a policeman?"

"One day too long." Sax frowned when he heard the sharp edge in his voice, but he didn't apologize.

She gave him another one of those long, probing looks. "Still, I find it difficult to believe that anyone who'd worn a badge for any length of time could turn off feelings of responsibility and the desire to protect others the way you can a water tap."

The answering look Sax gave her was cold. Hard. "Believe it."

With that clipped statement, he turned on his heel and left the room. A moment later Madeline heard the sound of water running in the adjoining room.

What a mess.

Sinking down on the bed, she dragged her hands through her hair, sighed deeply, and wished she knew who she was.

And what the hell it was that she'd gotten herself into.

IT WAS RAINING. A not unusual occurrence in this part of the country, certainly, but the slate gray clouds hovering over the city did nothing to improve the man's mood.

"Are you telling me that the boat sank?"

An underling, clad in a tailored navy blue suit, hovered nervously just inside the doorway. "Yes, sir. In the storm."

The gray-haired man scowled as he took a gold cigar clipper from the pocket of his vest and clipped the end off a dark cigar. "And when did you learn of this unfortunate accident?"

"Ah, last night, sir."

"Last night." He drew the cigar beneath his aristocratic nose, inhaling the rich, pungent scent of dried tobacco.

The younger man cleared his throat. "Well, technically this morning. It was after midnight when we picked up the coast guard transmission. I didn't think you'd want to be awakened."

"I see." He stuck the cigar between his lips and waited. The younger man rushed forward, pulled a lighter from his jacket pocket and lit it. "You didn't think I'd want to be awakened," he repeated on a puff of blue smoke.

"There were only two survivors," the other man said quickly. "And neither of them were the woman."

"Has the coast guard recovered her body?"

"No, sir. But the storm's stalled off the coast, and they can't begin any major search attempt until it passes."

"And you're assuming that she's dead."

"It certainly looks that way, sir. That water's ice-cold, not to mention all the rip tides and the rocks, and the boat was nearly two miles offshore when it started taking on water. I don't see how she could have possibly survived."

"But we won't know that, will we? Until her body shows up, my life is hanging by the damn flimsy thread of your assumption."

He puffed thoughtfully as he glared out the rain-streaked window. From this vantage point, high above the city, he could see the shipyards where his father had labored as a welder until his death, and where he'd been expected to end up, as well.

But he'd escaped his humble roots to enter a world of wealth and privilege and executive power. He traveled in limousines and private jets, and some of the most important men in the world routinely called on him for advice.

Everything had been going precisely according to plan. Until one inquisitive female had appeared from out of the blue, sticking her nose in places where it definitely didn't belong.

"Find her," he instructed brusquely.

"Yes, sir," the younger man answered on cue. "We'll locate the woman, sir," he said. "Don't worry." With that he was gone, closing the hand-carved oak office door behind him.

The man sat in his penthouse office, smoking and brooding. Madeline Delaney had been nothing but trouble from the beginning. The damn bitch was like a hand grenade with the pin pulled.

And she was rolling around his feet.

3

SAX VIOLENTLY TWISTED the faucet handles and cursed whoever it was who'd dumped Maddy whatever-her-name-was in his lap.

Obviously, going without a woman for too long made a man do foolish, uncharacteristic things. Like allowing a nervous female to order him around with his own unloaded revolver rather than take the risk of upsetting her by taking the damn gun away the moment he entered the room and found it pointed at his chest.

It was also becoming apparent that celibacy made a man think ridiculous thoughts. Like wishing he had some perfumed salts to add to Maddy's bathwater.

On the other hand, Sax decided with a grim smile, the woman had definitely piqued his interest. Along with a sharp curiosity he would have sworn had died along with his partner—and best friend—eighteen months ago.

Sax frowned. He didn't want to consider the ramifications of these renewed feelings. The last thing on earth he wanted, or could afford, was to get involved with anyone. Especially a woman who was so obviously in need of a man's protection.

The irony was that living a hermit's existence out here, on the very edge of the world, tended to give a man plenty of time to think about the last things on earth.

"That's what you get, pal," he muttered as he retrieved a clean towel from the hall cupboard. "Next time you feel like playing Sir Galahad, why don't you just settle for washing off some stupid sea gull's wings?"

At least rescuing a petroleum-slick sea gull would be harmless. Once it was cleaned off, Sax could simply send the bird on its way. He had the vague, threatening feeling that getting rid of the defenseless woman currently ensconced in his bedroom would be easier said than done.

Not that she was entirely defenseless. Sax sat on the edge of the tub, watched the water rise, and remembered how ferociously she'd battled when she'd mistaken him for her attacker. The woman was definitely a great deal tougher than she appeared.

She was also pleasingly soft and supple. His body stirred at the memory of how she'd felt lying atop him. He wondered if Maddy might display that same soft feminine sweetness during sex. Or would she make love like she fought—wild and maddening and definitely challenging?

Sax twisted the faucets shut and had started to leave the bathroom when he caught a glimpse of himself in the mirror over the sink. As he absently ran his fingers down the red lines her fingernails had left on his cheek, Sax remembered how, during the long and torturous night, he'd been struck by a strange, unbidden and entirely atypical feeling of masculine possessiveness.

What would happen, he had wondered as the deep purple shadows slowly surrendered to a frail, silvery predawn light, if, having found this lissome siren washed ashore onto his rocks, he simply kept her?

In all the months Sax had been living on the coast, loneliness had never been a problem. On the contrary, he enjoyed his solitude and had become stoically satisfied with his life. Being alone had become so natural for him that on those two brief trips he had made into Portland, he'd found himself desperately counting the hours until he could escape back to his isolated lighthouse.

He'd forgotten how incessantly loud city noises could be: the steady hum of traffic, the impatient blare of automobile horns, the strident wail of sirens.

And the people were always in such a hurry. Everyone seemed imbued with a frantic sense of purpose, as if they were destined to spend every waking hour in overdrive and were incapable of keeping their eyes off the clocks and watches that were inexorably ticking away their lives.

They even talked too rapidly. Sometimes, during the rapid intercourse of contract negotiations, it would seem as if they were speaking a different language. During those times, Sax's mind would wander back to the peaceful solitude of the coast.

When he'd eventually drag his mind back to the present, he'd find Ellen, who never missed a thing, glaring at him knowingly. Of all the women he'd ever known, his former wife had always been the only one capable of making him feel like a seven-year-old.

On his last trip, Ellen had taken him to lunch at a trendy seafood restaurant on the riverfront. It had been four days before Christmas, and the restaurant—a former cannery—had been festively decorated for the holiday season with a towering fragrant balsam trimmed in red velvet ribbons and colorful hand-blown glass balls. Fairy lights had twinkled amid the leaves of the room's healthy green plants, and in the corner of the restaurant, on a raised platform, an attractive young woman wearing a white silk blouse trimmed in red and a long red-and-green-plaid skirt had played Christmas carols on a gleaming ebony grand piano.

The wine, an Oregon chardonnay, had been crisp and dry; the salmon had been poached to perfection and seasoned with capers.

But rather than taking the time to enjoy the excellent meal or the palatable wine, or even the dazzling view of snowcapped Mount Hood hovering over the city outside the restaurant's wall of garland-trimmed windows, his former wife had continued to take business calls on her damn cellular telephone and cast furtive, anxious glances at the slim gold watch he'd remembered buying her for their first wedding anniversary.

All around them, the rest of the diners, laden with overstuffed shopping bags embossed with the names of the city's finest shops, seemed no more willing to relax and enjoy a respite from their frenzied holiday shopping. *Hurry, hurry. Rush, rush.* If there had been silver bells playing outside on the city sidewalks, Sax had doubted that anyone would have paused long enough to hear—let alone enjoy—them.

By the time he and Ellen had parted on the antique brick sidewalk in front of the restaurant—a mere thirty minutes after her rushed, customarily late arrival—Sax hadn't been able to conceal his relief.

From the riverfront, he'd driven directly to the gleaming glass-and-chrome condo that had once, in another lifetime, been his home, repacked his duffel bag, then left the city, racing through the slanting icy rain, breaking every speeding law on the Oregon statutes on his way back to Satan's Cove.

Would he have been in such a hurry to return if Maddy had been in Portland with him? Sax found himself wondering now. If he'd returned from lunch with his former wife to find this sexy little siren waiting in his king-size bed, wearing nothing but her snug white cotton T-shirt, bikini panties and a delicious, come-hither smile, would he have been willing to stay another night? A week? A lifetime?

"Hell." Cursing his suddenly overvivid imagination, he left the bathroom and marched back down the stairs, vowing to keep his mind on the matter at hand.

But although he fought against it as he slammed around the compact kitchen, making a breakfast he was no longer hungry for, he kept envisioning making love to a remarkably responsive Madeline on the rug in front of the black granite fireplace in the condo's bedroom.

Her hair would tumble over her bare shoulders, her breasts would fit perfectly into his palms; her rosy nipples would pebble like dark berries beneath the erotic onslaught of his teeth, his tongue. Her supple body would be warm and welcoming; her arms and legs would wrap around him, urging him into her warm silken sheath. She'd say his name over and over, in soft, ragged whispers, begging him to take her.

Sax closed his eyes, picturing her as she'd appear, her golden flesh gleaming in the glow of the orange firelight, while a soft Portland rain streamed down the foggy windowpane of his condominium window. Her soft lips, bruised a dark dusky rose from shared kisses, would be parted, and her doe brown eyes would open wide in feminine wonder as he claimed her totally.

Swearing violently, Sax opened his eyes and shook his head in self-disgust. Stomping over to the refrigerator, he took out a carton of eggs, vowing to keep his mind on the task at hand. But as he cracked an egg into the waffle mix with more strength than necessary, shattering the thin brown shell, provocatively sensual images of the woman who was currently upstairs, wet and naked in his bathtub, continued to burn in Sax's mind and in his loins.

AFTER LISTENING to the sound of his booted heels descending the stairway, Maddy pushed herself to her feet and limped into the bathroom across the narrow hallway.

The room definitely belonged to a man; there were no flowers on the walls, no pastel soaps, no delicate dishes containing potpourri, no pretty embroidered guest towels.

What there was was an ancient bathtub—clean, but showing signs of rust through the porcelain—a single bar of green deodorant soap, a navy blue washcloth tossed over the brass faucets and a thick brown towel folded atop the closed commode. The brown cotton mat in front of the tub was faded and well-worn.

After lowering herself gingerly into the steaming water, Madeline began scrubbing her aching body with the rough cloth until her bruised flesh glowed pink. While it hurt to wash so vigorously, the resultant pain reminded her that she was alive. Thanks to her dark, dispassionate host.

She leaned her head against the curved back of the lion-footed tub and closed her eyes. Although she had no memory of anything other than her name, and the strange, almost surrealistic image of Sax bringing her back to life on those rocks, she had absolutely no difficulty conjuring up his rigid, harshly hewn features.

He was tall, and lean—no, spare, she corrected—with a rangy, athletic build. Saxon Carstairs would have been an imposing cop; he exuded a cool confidence and power befitting a man who possessed such a hard body, strong mind and, she suspected, a rigid, unbending nature.

She wondered what had happened to make him leave the police force. Obviously, from his grittily issued response about having been a cop for one day too long, it had not been a very pleasant departure. Was the reason for his leaving his career the same thing that had caused him to turn his back on city life? Was it why he was living an isolated existence on the far edge of the continent?

Was it the same thing that had drained all the life from the man?

"Now you're getting downright fanciful," Madeline muttered, running the washcloth briskly down her arm. She flinched as it passed over the deep bruises on her wrist. The bruises were in the same place on her other wrist, mute evidence that her hands must have been tied at some time before she took her near-fatal swim in the sea.

"Perhaps he was an unemotional person to begin with," she argued with herself. "You have no reason to believe that he was ever any different than he appears right now."

Lifting her right leg, she scrubbed vigorously at the grains of salt that continued to cling stubbornly to her flesh.

"Perhaps he just doesn't like women. Perhaps he was treated badly by a woman at some time. Or maybe he just doesn't find them attractive. At least, not in any sexual way."

It didn't matter. Whether he distrusted all women because of some past unhappy experience or was gay or merely lacked passion, Madeline decided that she was definitely in no immediate danger alone in this lighthouse with the man.

"Besides," she insisted, turning her attention to her left leg, "you shouldn't be wasting time thinking about Saxon Carstairs when you've got your own missing life to figure out."

Since it was the only personal memory she had, Madeline returned her mind to that oddly surrealistic scene of watching Sax work furiously to save her life. Although she now knew that the mental image was not a dream, she felt oddly detached from the event. It was as if she were watching not herself, but someone else.

Sax's hands, pressed firmly against her chest, were strong and determined. Indeed, Madeline realized, if he were not such a stubborn man, she'd never have awakened in his bed this morning. Because she'd be dead.

She'd thought she was going to die, she remembered. Correction—for that brief, fleeting moment, she had actually ceased to exist. But Sax, refusing to allow her to surrender to death, had brought her back.

She vaguely remembered fighting him; she'd been terrified and had struck out in blind panic. But rather than strike her back, he'd soothed her, she recalled now. With words and a steady, reassuring touch of his hands.

Although there was no shower fixture, a flexible spray had been added to the tub. Turning it on, Madeline began to wash the grit from her hair with the tube of shampoo Sax had thoughtfully left for her. The dark green gel smelled like an evergreen forest; as she massaged the frothy suds through her hair, the suddenly familiar scent caused another all-too-vivid memory to flood back.

She remembered lying in Sax's bed. But she hadn't been alone. Madeline recalled Sax lying beneath her, trying to calm her violent struggles. She remembered inarticulate words, meant to comfort, crooned in her ear. Even now she could practically feel the strong, soothing touch of his broad hands moving down her bare back, over her hips, drawing her closer into his warmth. She remembered being sprawled indecorously over him, her legs draped over his thighs, her lips pressed against his neck.

Her last memory, as she had finally drifted back into a restless sleep, was of the green-forest scent emanating from his dark hair teasing her senses.

"Oh, no, that's what he meant," she groaned. "When he said I'd driven him crazy all night." She had a sudden urge to sink below the water and stay there. For the rest of her life.

But since that was impossible, Madeline eventually rinsed the evocatively scented suds out of her hair, then turned off the hand-held spray and rose from the tub.

Her damp skin, rosy from her earlier energetic scrubbing, seemed to scream in protest when she began to rub herself dry with the towel. Flinching, she patted her bruised flesh delicately, trying not to notice that she looked as if she'd been run over by a fishing trawler. The mirror was fogged from the hot steam that had risen from her bath. She rubbed it clear with the corner of the towel and groaned when she viewed her reflection. No wonder Sax had failed to display even the slightest bit of masculine interest, she considered bleakly.

She was, to put it charitably, a mess. Her red-rimmed eyes had dark shadows, like additional bruises beneath them, and there was an angry scarlet scrape running up her cheek. Another large purplish bruise marred her forehead. Her complexion bore a pallor she hoped wasn't natural, and she found herself wishing for a bright lipstick and a little rose blush.

At least she no longer looked like something the cat had dragged in from a swamp, Madeline concluded. She'd washed an amazing amount of sand down the drain, and her hair was squeaky clean.

She looked around the compact bathroom for a blow dryer and when she didn't immediately locate one, decided that it would take too long to dry her hair anyway. Especially since she was starving, and the aromas drifting up the stairs from the kitchen were practically making her mouth water.

On cue, her stomach growled. She dressed hastily in her freshly laundered clothing, gave herself one last judicious perusal in the mirror, frowned, then bit her lips and tried to pinch a little color into her cheeks. Finally, telling herself that he'd already seen her at her worst, she left the bathroom and followed the alluring scents down the curving staircase.

He'd obviously heard her coming. The moment she entered the kitchen, he handed her a mug of hot, steaming coffee.

He made a slow appraisal of her, from the top of her head down to her sneakers. Although his expression remained as unreadable as ever, Madeline thought she saw a flash of something that resembled banked anger flare in those steely eyes when they took in the vivid scrape along her cheek.

Surprisingly, for such a slender woman, she filled out the crimson sweater very well; remembering how his body had reacted to the sight of those pert breasts beneath that little white undershirt, Sax felt another renewed twinge of desire. Her jeans were attractively snug, hugging hips that were slender but femininely curved.

"You're looking better."

"I clean up well," she said with a quick, appealing grin that made him feel as if the sun had suddenly come from out behind the slate gray clouds. He stared at that smile for a long moment, mesmerized by its warmth.

"Well, you definitely look like you're going to live," he said finally.

"Thanks to you."

"I told you, I didn't have any choice after you washed up on my rocks."

"Still," she insisted, "it was very kind of you."

"Don't be so quick to misrepresent the situation. I'm never kind."

Not knowing exactly how to answer that, Madeline blew on the coffee to cool it slightly, then took a tentative sip. It was hot and strong and as dark as midnight. "You know," she mused, "You never did tell me what you were doing out there on the beach in the first place."

Sax shrugged and returned his attention to the cast-iron frying pan where bacon sizzled hotly. "I was taking a walk."

"At night? In the middle of a storm?"

"It wasn't night yet."

"Still—"

"How do you want your eggs?" he asked brusquely in what Madeline realized was a not very subtle attempt to change the subject.

Intrigued by his fleeting irritation—any emotion was better than none at all—she decided to continue questioning him. "However you're having yours is fine. Do you always walk in storms?"

"Sometimes." He took the bacon out of the pan, put it on a paper towel to drain, then poured the grease into a nearby coffee can. "Do you want one egg or two?"

"One's plenty."

"Over easy okay?"

"Fine. Why?"

Sax broke three eggs into the frying pan. "Why, what?"

"Why do you walk in storms?"

"Are you always this damn inquisitive?" Sax muttered through gritted teeth.

"I don't know," Madeline answered honestly. "But I think I probably am."

"Just my luck." He flipped the eggs with a restraint of motion she found momentarily fascinating. "Of all the mermaids in the sea, I have to catch myself a talkative one."

For some reason she could not quite discern, she rather liked his calling her a mermaid. It made her feel that perhaps he didn't consider her as hopelessly unattractive as she was finding herself.

"It just seems that most people would probably want to stay indoors when the weather's so bad," she probed.

He shrugged again. "I'm not most people."

Now that she could believe. Realizing that getting any information from this man would be like pulling teeth, she fell silent.

Outside, the storm continued to rage; inside the kitchen, it was warm and cozy. Beginning to relax, albeit only slightly, Madeline sipped her coffee, watching with admiration as he managed to cook breakfast with a proficiency that most short-order cooks would have admired. For such a large man, he moved with a remarkable catlike grace. There were no unexpected or unnecessary actions. When Sax did move, Madeline noticed, it was with definite purpose.

Once again she remembered the feel of those deft hands moving down her bare back. Embarrassed color flooded into her cheeks, and she looked away.

Sax didn't miss the vivid blush staining her cheeks. "What are you thinking about right now?"

The sudden question, grittily asked, garnered her reluctant attention. "Nothing."

"Now who's the liar?" he taunted softly.

The color deepened, turning her face as scarlet as a summer sunset. "It's not important."

"How can you know that?" he argued. He slid the eggs onto two plates, along with the bacon, and placed them on the pine trestle table. "Your memory's like a jigsaw puzzle, Maddy. Every little piece, no matter how seemingly unimportant, eventually fits together to create a whole picture."

He took another two plates piled high with fat Belgium waffles out of the warming oven and placed them on the table with the first, along with a bottle of maple syrup. "More coffee?"

"Just a bit." Maddy held out her mug. "It's very good."

"Most women find it too strong," he volunteered as he topped off the chipped white mug.

"I'm not most women," she said evenly.

Sax liked the way she'd twisted his own words and threw them back at him. Their eyes met in an unspoken challenge.

Her calm, brandy-colored eyes dueled silently with his hard, iron-hued ones, neither wanting to be the first to look away. Myriad emotions swirled between them: irritation, frustration, curiosity, and then he saw something else.

Anticipation was written over her face in bold, unmistakable strokes.

Telling himself that he was playing with fire, Sax let his gaze leave her eyes to brush over her mouth, lingering on her lips. Against all reason, he found himself imagining the taste and feel of those softly bruised lips beneath his own.

As if answering some unspoken command, they parted slightly on a soft sigh. When he reluctantly returned his gaze to her eyes, he saw both surprise and a rising, reluctant desire.

In that suspended moment, they both knew that he only need reach out and touch her—a hand to her cheek, a fingertip to her parted lips—to change everything.

He lifted his hand slightly, as if to do exactly that. She leaned toward him. Then, at the last possible moment, common sense intervened. Just in time he dropped his hand to his side.

"No," he said. "You're not like other women. Whoever you are, mermaid, you are definitely one of a kind."

The gritty yet coolly unemotional tone was back. The heat that had flared so seductively in his eyes was carefully banked. The sensual mood had disintegrated like early-morning fog over the sea.

In fact, Madeline considered, if it weren't for the fact that his hands were now curled into tight fists, as if to keep them from temptation, she might have thought that she had imagined the entire suspended moment.

"Is it me?" she asked quietly. "Or is it all women?"

Damning himself for almost losing control that way, Sax pulled her chair out for her. "I don't know what you're talking about."

She remained standing and looked up into his rigid face. "Don't you?"

"No." His expression had turned laconic, even slightly derisive, warning her to stop.

"It's just that while I was taking my bath, it crossed my mind that perhaps you'd had a bad experience with a woman at one time," she probed. "Or maybe," she added, "you simply might not like women. In that way."

Deciding that she must possess a reckless streak, she ignored the warning in his sharp gaze. "I decided that perhaps I shouldn't take personally the fact that you didn't seem to like me."

"Other than getting stood up for the homecoming dance in the tenth grade, I haven't had any real ego-deflating experiences in the male-female department. And just to set the record straight, I like women," Sax assured her roughly. "In the right place. At the right time."

"Ah, a chauvinist," she said on a nod. "I should have figured it out when you told me you were a cop."

"I'm not a cop. I quit."

"That's right." She gave him a sweet, false smile. "I seem to recall you mentioning something about that."

Determined to create some sort of reaction and needing to touch him, as he'd been about to touch her, she reached up and ran her fingertip along the angry red lines on his cheek. "Did I do that?"

The only answer to her question was stony silence. He looked down at her with that silent, brooding stare Madeline was beginning to hate.

"I did, didn't I?" Unable to resist, she trailed her fingers down the side of his rigid face. A muscle tensed tautly beneath her touch, but she refused to take her hand away. "I'm sorry."

He remained statue-still, and his hooded eyes revealed absolutely no emotion. What kind of a man was Sax Carstairs? Madeline wondered. And what would it take for a woman to get beneath that iron-clad control?

Intrigued, she decided to test him further. "It was a terrible way to reward the man who'd gone out in the storm to rescue me." Watching his face carefully, she ran her fingers slowly, tantalizingly from his earlobe down the strong, forbidding jawline.

Amazing. There was still absolutely no sign of emotional involvement on his part.

"But I forgot," she murmured silkily. "You didn't go out specifically to rescue me at all, did you, Sax?" Madeline was finding it to be a strangely heady experience, being the sexual aggressor. Being the one in control. "You were just out for an evening stroll on the coast, during a near typhoon, when you stumbled across me lying there like a piece of beached driftwood." She didn't believe that. Not for a minute.

Growing even more intrepid, not to mention increasingly frustrated, she traced a path down his corded neck with her fingernails.

"You know," he said, his voice rumbling like the distant crash of waves on the rocky shore, "if you keep this up, mermaid, you might just get more than you bargained for."

Success! She'd finally made him speak.

The gritty male tone revealed that she was capable of causing a degree of havoc to his senses, that this alien heat flowing through her veins was not hers alone. It was enough. For now.

She'd already decided that she'd pushed her luck far enough when unwelcome reality came crashing down on her, leaving her both shocked and appalled at her behavior. There were names for women who led men on with sexual innuendo, as she'd just done. None of them attractive. And although she couldn't remember anything about her past, Madeline knew without a doubt that such behavior was definitely atypical.

She pulled her hand away from his flesh, as if burned.

"Oh, God. I'm sorry." She sank onto the wooden chair and buried her flaming face in her hands. "I can't imagine what got into me."

"How about stress, along with a little natural sexual curiosity?" Sax suggested on a calm, rigorously controlled tone that did not reveal the fires her teasing touch had kindled inside him. "After all, we did spend the night together."

She dropped her hands from her flaming face to the table; her startled gaze flew guiltily to his expressionless face.

"So you did remember that much," Sax said. He felt a certain satisfaction in knowing that she hadn't forgotten everything.

Madeline licked her suddenly too dry lips, then wished she hadn't when a burst of unrestrained passion flared in his eyes.

"I remember you saving my life," she said quietly. "And I remember fighting you. And . . ." Her soft voice drifted off.

"And?"

"Nothing." She shook her head, looked down at the pine surface of the table again and began tracing the outline of a dark pine knot with her fingernail.

"What else?"

"I told you, nothing else."

He caught her downcast chin in his fingers, lifting her embarrassed gaze to his. "Then let me refresh your memory about last night, Maddy," he said, his deep voice surrounding her like a caress. "Let me tell you how damn good you felt lying on top of me, all warm and soft and nearly naked."

"I felt safe." It was the truth. She remembered, once she'd stopped struggling, that she'd never felt so protected in her life.

"You shouldn't have. Because while you were wiggling that sexy little body against mine all night, I was going out of my mind. I was also wishing that I didn't have too many scruples just to take you right then and there and end my torment."

"You would have actually taken advantage of me while I was sleeping?"

It was then that he surprised her, giving her a slow, sexy grin that took years off his age and started her pulse racing. "If I had been ungentlemanly enough to take advantage of your helpless condition and make love to you, believe me, mermaid, you wouldn't have remained asleep."

She definitely believed that.

Madeline stared at Sax, transfixed by the sudden emotion swirling in his eyes. Eyes that had become the deep color of wood smoke. She'd been all wrong about this man, she realized belatedly. He wasn't the slightest bit dispassionate. He wasn't at all cold.

And he definitely wasn't safe.

She'd wanted to garner an emotion—any emotion—from Saxon Carstairs and she'd succeeded. But every feminine instinct she possessed told her that the lambent heat gleaming in his gaze could be infinitely dangerous.

"Breakfast is getting cold," he said.

On impulse, he, a man who never gave in to impulse, ran the roughened pad of his thumb down her still-flushed cheek. Her skin was soft and silky and eminently touchable. "Eat up, mermaid. Something tells me that you're going to need all your strength before this is through."

For some reason she refused to contemplate while her nerves were so on edge, his voice reminded her of the waves beating against the rocks outside the lighthouse—dark, deep and potentially dangerous.

As he dived into his breakfast, Madeline couldn't quite decide whether to take his words as a promise or a threat.

4

AFTER BREAKFAST, during which they exchanged fewer than ten words, Sax curtly instructed Madeline to leave the dishes for him to do later.

He needed to think. And he couldn't do that with her sitting across the table, watching him warily through her thick lashes, looking as if he was going to leap out of his chair, grab her by her still-damp hair and drag her upstairs to his bed.

Which wouldn't be all that bad an idea. She'd nearly driven him over the edge with that reckless stunt earlier, running her slender fingers down his face, playing with his ear, scraping her nails against the warming flesh of his neck as if she didn't even realize that she was playing with fire.

She was either the bravest, the most naive or the most idiotic woman he'd ever had the misfortune to meet, Sax decided as he marched through the pelting rain to the rocky tide pool where he'd pulled his sexy, maddening mermaid from the sea.

What the hell had she thought she was doing, playing sexual games with a man she didn't even know? How had she known that he wouldn't take her up on her provocative offer, forcing himself on her, right then and there, on top of the kitchen table?

Not that he would have had to use force, Sax determined. He had, after all, seen that same heat that had been searing through his veins gleaming in her warm, brandy-colored eyes.

So why hadn't he seized the moment and eased the ache that had been torturing his body ever since he'd made the mistake of climbing into bed with the woman?

Because, he answered his own rhetorical question, he'd saved her life. And by doing that, he'd earned her trust, whether he wanted it or not. So now it was his responsibility to see that he didn't breach that trust. No matter how difficult the next few hours—or days, he considered, glaring out at the black clouds that seemed to have stalled over the jetty—might be.

"This is where you found me, isn't it?"

The soft voice, coming from directly behind him, startled Sax out of his frustrated thoughts. He spun around to see her standing a few feet away, dwarfed in the olive green rain poncho that had been hanging beside the kitchen door when he left the house.

He was definitely losing his touch, Sax decided grimly, when a rank amateur could sneak up on him. "You're going to catch pneumonia, coming out in the cold and rain like this," he warned.

She shrugged, the motion barely perceptible beneath the heavy waterproof fabric. "I'm a lot hardier than I look."

She looked down into the tide pool, catching a fleeting glimpse of a spiny sea urchin amid the floating kelp and gleaming bits of agate and jasper. Just beyond the tide pool, the waves crashed against the rocks, sending up towering white plumes of spray.

"You didn't answer my question," she reminded him when he didn't say anything for a nerve-rackingly long time.

"Yes. This is where I found you."

"I think I recognize it."

She continued to stare down at the tide pool. Sax remained silent, watching. Waiting. After a time she slowly, almost tentatively lifted her gaze out to the storm-tossed sea.

There were dark shapes, like shadows moving through the whitecapped waves. "Whales," she breathed softly as she caught sight of an unmistakable plume of spray a long way offshore.

"They're migrating," he said, watching the faint memory stir in her eyes. "It's their annual trek from Baja to Alaska. I was photographing them when I first saw your boat."

"So you did come looking for me." She nodded but didn't take her eyes from the water. "I thought you must have." Images tugged at her memory. It was as if she were watching them through a thick veil of fog. Suddenly a brisk wind blew the fog away, and she had a startling, clear picture of herself standing on the deck of a wildly pitching boat, a very large and very ugly gun pointed directly at her.

"I was on that boat," she whispered, her voice nearly carried away by the sea wind. "With a man."

Sax drew nearer in order to hear her soft tone. "Can you recognize him?" he asked quietly, careful not to disturb her train of thought.

"No. I can see his face clearly," she said. "But I don't think I'd ever seen him before yesterday."

"Was there anyone else on the boat?"

"Two other men. But they stayed below deck. They were seasick," she recalled suddenly. "I remember thinking how strange it was that I wasn't sick—I'm usually a terrible sailor—but then I decided that I must have been too frightened."

"That makes sense." Sax concluded that she must at one time have lived by the sea to know that she was a bad sailor. But he decided to wait until later to interrogate her along those lines.

"Look around you," he suggested in a low, even voice. "You're on the deck of the boat. What do you see?"

"Oh!" Her eyes widened at the memory. "A whale. It was breaching itself right beside the boat."

It crossed his mind that he'd probably captured that precise moment on film and cursed himself for not thinking of it sooner. He was definitely slipping.

"That's when I dived overboard."

He considered the courage it would take to dive into that roiling sea and felt a tug of admiration.

"I knew it was risky," she said on a faraway voice that led him to believe that she was no longer with him, but out in that icy water. "But I knew that I didn't have any other choice. Because the man with the gun was going to kill me.

"But the water was so cold, colder than I ever imagined it could be, and I didn't know how far from shore I was." She drew in a deep, shuddering breath and began to tremble.

"My arms and legs were like stone weights, but I tried to keep swimming. Then I saw the lights and realized how far I still had to go, and it seemed hopeless."

Damn. He'd turned on the lights, hoping to offer whatever scant assistance he could. Knowing that all he'd done was discourage her was depressing.

As if reading his mind, Madeline said, "But they were still a big help because at least once I saw them, I knew what direction to try to swim in. I kept going under."

Her eyes widened farther; her gaze revealed a distant terror. "Just when I thought—no, when I knew—I was going to drown for sure . . ." Her voice trailed off, and she wrapped her arms around her trembling body in an unconscious gesture of self-protection.

It took an effort, but Sax resisted taking her into his arms. "What happened next?"

She looked up at him for the first time since beginning her story. "You'll think I'm crazy. Or at least hallucinating."

"The entire incident is crazy," he declared. "But that doesn't mean I don't believe you."

"There was a dolphin," she said at length. "It swam up to me and I grabbed hold of it, and it began pulling me toward shore."

"I've read of that happening," he said musingly. "But I've always thought it was myth."

"Me, too," Madeline agreed. "But it really, truly happened."

"I believe you. What next?" He thought he knew the story from here, but had to ask.

"I don't remember reaching these rocks," she said, returning her gaze to the tide pool. "But—and this is going to sound like I belong locked away in a padded room—but I remember watching you bring me back to life."

He quirked a dark brow. "Are you saying you had an out-of-body experience?"

She couldn't meet his gaze. "I know that sounds crazier than everything else I've said so far, but yes. I do.

"I saw you, Sax. And I saw myself. And you were pounding on my chest and breathing into my mouth and then you were cursing, telling me that you weren't going to let me die."

When she lifted her eyes to his, Sax viewed a soft sheen of moisture in the whiskey-colored depths. "And I honestly believe that it was your determination that made me come back," she said quietly. "You were so desperate and so angry, I couldn't imagine letting you down."

The silence lingered between them.

"I've been there," he said finally, just when Madeline thought she was going to implode from the tension building inside her.

Of all the things she'd expected him to say, never in a million years would she have expected that simple statement. "You have?"

"Yeah." The lines bracketing his mouth deepened. "I was shot in an undercover drug bust that went bad a year and a half ago," he revealed reluctantly.

She could sense from his remote expression and his emotionless tone that it was not in Sax's nature to share what had obviously been a horrendous experience.

"I remember seeing myself lying on the gurney in the emergency room while the doctors and nurses and paramedics were trying to bring me back to life."

"Which they obviously did."

He nodded, his lips drawn together in a grim line. "Only after I saw my partner's body. Nobody was working on him. He was too far gone.

"That's when I knew I had to come back. To make certain the bastard who'd caused a nice woman to be widowed and a pair of twins to be orphaned got what was coming to him."

Madeline had known, although he'd flatly denied it, that Sax was imbued with a deep sense of responsibility. She might not be able to remember who she was or what she was doing here in Satan's Cove, Oregon, but at least Sax's revelation assured her that her instincts about men—at least this man—were right on the mark.

Saxon Carstairs was a good man. A caring man. And she was already beginning to care for him, more than she should.

"And did he?" she asked quietly. "Get what was coming to him?"

It would have been impossible to miss the haunted look that came into his eyes. "The guy who pulled the trigger got life without parole," he said. "Which is a hell of a lot more than Brian got."

"Brian was your partner?"

"Yeah." Sax shook his head at the death of such a good man for such a small amount of deadly white powder. "We never got the guy who was running the operation."

His scowl darkened as he remembered, just before he'd received his near-fatal wounds, demanding that the dealer Brian had shot during the rapid exchange of gunfire tell him who he was working for. But the piece of scum hadn't cooperated, instead only muttering a ragged word that sounded like "paradise."

Sax recalled responding that it was too late for praying; the man's final destination was bound to be a great deal hotter and less comfortable. He'd no sooner gotten the words out than he caught a movement in his peripheral vision. Then an image of a man, clad all in black, holding an automatic rifle.

That was all he remembered. A moment later, the world had gone black.

Dragging his hand down his face, Sax forced his mind back to his conversation. "When I rejoined the living after my surgery and realized that I'd cheerfully kill the kingpin myself with my bare hands if I ever found him, I knew I'd stepped over some invisible line. The day I was released from the hospital, I quit the force and came here."

The pain in his voice tore at something elemental inside Madeline. Wanting—needing—to establish some type of physical link, she lifted her palm to his cheek.

Although there was a long moment of stillness, Sax didn't pull away.

"I'm glad," she murmured, her eyes on his. "Not that your partner died, of course, but that you lived. And you came here."

"To save you."

"Yes." She felt suddenly, strangely shy. "That, too."

Sax would have had to have been blind not to see the invitation swirling in her eyes; he would have had to have been deaf not to hear it in her soft tone. And he would have had to have been made of steel not to respond.

Slowly, deliberately, giving himself time to change his mind, giving her time to back away, Sax lowered his head.

When Sax touched his mouth to hers, Madeline sighed. When his teeth nipped at the delicate pink flesh of her lower lip, she moaned. Her fingers linked around his neck, drawing him closer.

And then he was lost.

He'd thought he'd known what he wanted, had believed he'd known what to expect. But he'd been wrong. Because the feel of her soft lips, her taste, rocked him all the way to the bone.

For all his intensity, the kiss was meltingly soft. His mouth tempted, enticed, seduced. At the first taste, passion exploded, wild and hot and free inside of Madeline. Her emotions were suddenly raw. She clung to him, mindlessly willing, desperately wanting.

Waves crashed against the rocks like thunder, echoing the out-of-control beat of her heart. A cold rain streamed down her uplifted face, but as his lips moved from her parted lips to blaze a flaming trail up her cheek, she felt her skin burn.

"Sax, please." She turned her head, anxious to have his mouth on hers again. What she wanted, Madeline realized, was to have Sax take her by storm. Once again she was finding his strong, waiting quality both intriguing and frustrating. "Kiss me again."

"That's what I'm doing." Without rushing, his mouth moved over her face. The hood of the poncho had fallen back. His lips nuzzled at her temple, her ear; his teeth tugged at her earlobe.

"No." She framed his face between her hands and dragged his mouth back to hers. "I mean, really kiss me."

When he obliged, finding her mouth with unerring accuracy, her arms went around him again, holding him close as her lips parted in avid demand. His hands tangled in her hair, his fingers raking through the thick wet strands.

Her lips were cool from the rain, but warmed quickly. Thunder boomed on the horizon; the wind picked up, and the rain continued to fall from the pewter gray clouds. Caught up in a whirling storm of her own, Madeline didn't notice. She was quickly discovering that pleasure this warm, this fluid, could not be contained. Feelings flooded over her; her senses were swimming with him. She felt as if she were drowning all over again.

But this time she didn't want to be saved.

They were pressed together so tightly that even the wind couldn't separate them. But he had to touch her. Despite all reason, despite every vestige of common sense and self-control Sax possessed, he knew that he'd go out of his mind if he couldn't have more.

She'd complained about his patience without knowing exactly how much that patience was costing him. He'd expected the pleasure, had known there would be passion. But he'd never expected such pain. For the first time in his life, his body ached for a woman; for the first time in memory, his blood burned. The heated blood was pounding in his head and in his veins. He managed to get his hands beneath the oversize poncho. Yanking her sweater up, he cupped her breasts in his palms.

She arched against him, murmuring his name even as she offered more. But the damn T-shirt was between them, tucked tightly into the waistband of her jeans. Frustrated, and needing to feel her silken flesh, he gripped the scooped neckline and tore the cotton away.

The sound of the material ripping was drowned out by the moan of the wind and Madeline's inarticulate sounds of approval.

She seemed so very small against him; she felt so very fragile. He could feel her heart pounding beneath his fingertips, and his hunger built with every frantic beat. Images rushed through his mind, images of making love to Maddy, provocative, tempestuous images that were every bit as dangerous as the storm-tossed sea he'd rescued her from.

He could take her now, he realized. Right here, on the rocks, in the storm, he could drag her to the wet, cold sand and before either of them would realize exactly how it had happened, he could be buried deep inside her, losing himself in her silken warmth, claiming her, possessing her even as he was possessed.

It would be so easy. It was so damn tempting. It was also so wrong.

Sax had always believed that lovemaking should be a shared experience of two equals. It was something that should not be forced. And it should definitely not be rushed.

Abruptly he tore his mouth from hers and buried it against her neck. After a long, aching moment, he drew back, shaken by the intensity of his visceral need for this woman.

"Sax?" Her eyes slowly fluttered open. They were wide and still vague with confused desire as she stared up at him. "I don't understand."

Shaken and determined not to show it, he put her a little away from him. "That makes two of us."

"But—"

He pressed his hand against her lips, forestalling any further questions. With hands that were not nearly as steady as he would have liked, Sax rearranged her clothing, frowning as he realized that he'd ruined that little undershirt he'd found so appealing. He'd never been so rough with a woman, never displayed such a lack of finesse.

"I'm sorry I tore your shirt."

Her shoulders moved in a faint shrug. "I can buy another."

He raked his hands through his hair, frustrated and ashamed. "I don't usually behave that way. I've never torn a woman's clothing."

She surprised him by dimpling at that. "Then we're even. Because I've never wanted a man to tear my clothing before. Until a minute ago." She put a reassuring hand on his arm. "I felt like I was going to go crazy if you didn't touch me."

He wanted her. That in itself was surprising because it had been a very long time since he'd wanted anything or anyone. What was even more stunning was the fact that she wanted him, too.

If the storm didn't pass soon, allowing him to take her to the mainland, it was inevitable that they'd both get what they wanted before their time together was over. Just as it was inevitable that they'd both pay. Nothing came without risks, Sax had determined long ago. And nothing was ever free.

"Well, you definitely weren't the only one going crazy." He pulled the hood of the poncho back over her wet hair. He left his own head bare so that the rain could cool his head and hopefully steady his pounding heart. "I'm not a man who makes many noble gestures, mermaid." Because he could not resist, Sax allowed the back of his hand to trail down the silken skin of her cheek. "This just happens to be one of them."

Deciding that discretion was the better part of valor, Madeline didn't challenge his curious statement. Instead, she remained as silent as he continued to be as they walked together back along the rocky, untamed beach littered with broken shells and silvery gray driftwood.

"I'm going upstairs to develop that roll of film I took yesterday," he informed her as they entered the lighthouse. "Hopefully it'll provide some answers."

"May I watch?"

He shot her a surprised look, then shrugged. "Suit yourself."

Well, it certainly wasn't a gilded invitation. But it wasn't a complete rejection, either. Deciding to take whatever she could get from this man, Madeline hung the poncho on the hook next to the door, beside his parka, and followed him out of the kitchen to the curving stairway.

When they reached the second-floor landing, she said, "I want to get a towel, to dry my hair."

"Fine." He didn't bother to stop.

Inwardly cursing herself for being the slightest bit interested in such an unpleasant individual, Madeline stomped into the bathroom, yanked the brown towel from the brass rack and began rubbing vigorously at her damp hair, trying not to remember how exactly it had gotten wet in the first place.

She yanked her sweater over her head, discarded the torn T-shirt, then put the sweater back on again. For the first time in her life, she was grateful that her breasts were too small to need the support of a bra.

She held the white cotton garment in her hand, remembering how she'd felt when he'd torn it, how excited she'd been. How aroused. She'd been hovering on the brink of madness, and it would have taken only the faintest push to send her plummeting over the edge. At the glorious, frightening, suspended moment in time, she would have gone. Willingly.

But just as she'd been about to give herself up to a passion she'd never felt before, he'd abruptly broken off the heated kiss and practically pushed her away from him. And although she'd jump back into that raging sea again before admitting it, Sax's behavior had left her wanting more. Much, much more.

It had also left her feeling horribly embarrassed. And ashamed.

And those were the feelings she needed to concentrate on, Madeline told herself. Like it or not, she was stuck here with a man who obviously wanted her but hated himself for the wanting.

The thing to do was not to think about that heated kiss, she told herself as she climbed up the curving stairs to the third floor. If she were to survive the next few hours before the storm passed—please God, she prayed silently, let it not be days—she had to concentrate on the pain, not the pleasure.

That blinding, shared kiss had been a horrendous mistake. One she couldn't allow to happen again.

5

MADELINE VOWED not to give in to her tumultuous feelings; she would not permit herself to remember how right his bold, hard mouth had felt on hers, how wonderful it had felt when he'd taken her in his arms. Sax Carstairs was only a man, like any other. She refused to allow him to make her feel so unsettled. So vulnerable. So desperate.

She gave herself that little pep talk all the way up to the third floor, where she found him in what was obviously a photo lab. "Nice setup," she said, looking around at what appeared to be expensive professional equipment.

There were a number of 35 mm camera bodies, along with a variety of interchangeable lenses, a Hasselblad medium-format camera, which she somehow knew to be a proven workhorse among professionals, cans of compressed air, tripods, a fluorescent light box, light meters, flash units, strobes and an enlarger. A double stainless-steel sink was against the wall, next to a pair of filing cabinets.

"I like it." He took the temperature of the chemicals, then ran a stream of warm water over the side of the developer to warm it.

"You took those photographs hanging on the wall in the bedroom, didn't you?"

"Guilty. Could you close the door, please?"

She did as requested. "They're very good."

His only answer to that was an inarticulate grunt as he poured the developer into the tank.

"Are you a professional photographer?"

"I guess you could call me that. Want to flick those wall switches behind you?"

The minute she flicked the first one down, the room was plunged into darkness. At the second, the low, cool sounds of a jazz saxophone filtered from some hidden speakers.

Sax opened a black plastic canister, slid out the roll of film, loaded it onto the reel and placed it in the developing tank.

"From a big-city cop to a professional photographer is quite a career change. I'm impressed."

"Don't be. You haven't seen any of my checks."

"I'd imagine making a living in the arts takes time. But you'll make it."

"Ah. Perhaps you're an art critic?"

Deciding not to take the edge in his tone seriously, Madeline merely smiled and said, "I don't think so."

She perched atop a nearby stool, rubbing her hair dry with the towel as Sax developed the rolls of film. He worked well in the dark. As soon as each roll of negatives was developed, he'd pull the cord that flooded the room with an amber, unearthly glow, put the film in the stop bath, the fix, the hypo, then the wash, before beginning the sequence all over again.

He moved around the darkroom as he had in the kitchen while cooking their breakfast. His motions were fluid, apparently effortless, but never careless, imbued with a tight control Madeline was beginning to suspect was second nature.

Her vow not to permit herself any sensual thoughts toward this man disintegrated as she found herself wondering if Sax would maintain that same rigid self-control while making love.

She didn't think so. From the power she'd sensed surging beneath the surface when he'd kissed her, Madeline had the feeling that if he ever allowed his tightly held passion free rein, the resultant explosion would rival a volcano. Which is precisely what he reminded her of, she considered. Heat and steam simmering dangerously beneath the surface of a cool, sometimes icy exterior.

He would be an aggressive, demanding lover, she decided. But she sensed that he'd be tender, too. She also had the vague, unsettling feeling that before all this was over, despite any vow she might make, the beguiling combination of strength and tenderness would prove impossible to resist.

Lost in his work, Sax remained oblivious to Madeline's sensuous thoughts. After he'd gone through the process five times, he finally found what he was looking for. "Here we go," he said with satisfaction. "I think this is the right roll."

She came over to stand beside him, studying the negatives through the magnifying loupe he handed her. She couldn't make out any boat.

"I'll make a contact sheet and see what we've got," he said.

Without being asked, Madeline, anxious to do something to assist in solving her own mystery, went over to a nearby shelf, opened a yellow box and took out the proper-size paper.

"You definitely know your way around a photo lab," Sax murmured, watching her with interest.

The action had been instinctive. Now, giving it some thought, Madeline paused, looking down at the resin-coated photographic paper she was holding.

"Perhaps you're a photographer." Grabbing up one of the cameras, he thrust it into her hand. "Here. Try this out."

Eager for some clue as to her identity, Madeline willingly obliged him by looking through the lens. "It feels almost as awkward as the gun did," she said with a sad little sigh.

"Are you sure?" He needn't have asked. She was holding the camera as if she was afraid it was going to bite.

"Positive."

The defeated slump of her slender shoulders moved him in a way that was definitely too dangerous for comfort. Knowing that he was taking an inordinate risk, he took the camera out of her hands, returned it to the shelf and then drew her into his arms.

"Perhaps you work in a photo lab," he suggested.

Drawing comfort from the feel of his strong arms around her, Madeline rested her forehead against the firm line of his shoulders. "I don't think so," she murmured into his navy blue sweatshirt. "It felt a lot more natural just sitting on that stool, watching you work."

"Perhaps you have a friend who's a photographer. Or a lover." Something that felt uncomfortably like jealousy moved through Sax.

A memory flickered, like the disjointed flash of a strobe light. "Channing," she murmured. "I used to watch Channing develop his film."

"Channing who?"

"Channing . . ." She paused, struggling for the name that was on the tip of her tongue. "Damn. I can't remember." She shook her head in frustration. "How could I forget the name of the man who—" Suddenly realizing what she had been about to say, Madeline clamped her jaw shut. Hard.

She knew she hadn't been fast enough when Sax's hold on her tightened. "Who what?"

She closed her eyes and wished that an earthquake would open up and swallow up the jetty and the lighthouse, including this darkroom and her right along with it. "I don't remember."

She was lying. Cupping her chin between his fingers, Sax lifted her reluctant gaze to his. The amber overhead light turned the bruises on her face the hue of dark ripe plums. "I think you do."

Although she'd only known him a few hours, Madeline could already recognize that stubborn, patient look. She knew that Sax was prepared to wait until doomsday for the truth.

"He was my first lover, all right?" she flared, pulling away for him. "Channing Mathison was a photographer I met when I was still in college and I fell head over heels in love with him. I thought he was in love with me, but after the summer was over, I never heard from him again."

Her hands were splayed on her hips, and sparks practically radiated around her. "Is that what you wanted to hear? Does it make you feel superior to know that some man I followed around for three months like a cocker spaniel puppy dumped me?"

Jealousy at the idea of some other man making love to his mermaid warred with the primitive urge to smash the bastard's face in for having hurt her. With an iron control that had always served him well, Sax reined in both emotions and stuck to the more immediate problem. "You said his last name was Mathison?"

She was surprised to have said it. "That's right. It was."

"And he was a photographer?"

"He was on the faculty at the Brooks Institute," Madeline said without thinking. The minute those words were out of her mouth, she realized that her past was beginning to come back. She stared at Sax in surprise.

"Now we're getting somewhere." Sax nodded, satisfied and encouraged.

The world-famous Brooks Institute, in Santa Barbara, California, offered a variety of degrees in professional photography. It also conducted workshops several times throughout the year.

In fact, Sax had cashed in several savings bonds he'd inherited from his maiden aunt and taken a few of the courses himself—on outdoor scenic photography, wildlife photography and darkroom techniques—during his vacations while on the force. It had been at one of those workshops that he'd met Ellen, but he didn't feel the need to mention that little fact.

He tried to remember a faculty member named Channing Mathison and came up blank.

"Are you from Santa Barbara?" That would explain her tan, he considered.

She thought about that for a minute. "I don't think so. Not now, anyway."

"But you've obviously been there. During one summer."

"Obviously." Madeline combed her fingers through her hair. "I know!" Her eyes brightened with the light of memory.

She slipped from his arms and began pacing around the small tower room. "It was the summer after my sophomore year at Northwestern. I was a journalism major and I thought it might be a good idea to take a photography course, since I figured I'd probably have to start out on the type of small paper that made reporters take their own photos."

"That explains what you were doing in Santa Barbara with good old Chauncy."

"Channing."

Sax definitely didn't like the way her voice softened when she said the jerk's name. And she'd gotten a far-away look in her eyes that was beginning to irritate the hell out of him. "Channing, Chauncy, whatever. The guy's name isn't important. Northwestern is in Illinois. Is that where you're from?"

"No." She stopped in front of the developing trays, looking down into the chemicals as if watching a picture slowly develop. "In fact, until orientation week my freshman year, I'd never been out of California. I thought I'd freeze to death before I could go home to L.A. for Christmas vacation."

"So you're from Los Angeles."

"Yes." Her smile matched the light in her eyes. The name of the Southern California city was comfortingly familiar. "Actually I grew up in Santa Monica, but I don't think I've lived there for quite a while." The smile slowly faded, replaced by a frown as she tried to remember more.

"Don't worry, it'll come," Sax assured her, brushing at the lines furrowing her brow with his fingertips. "In its own time. Let's go back to what you do remember—college... Northwestern isn't cheap," he reflected. "You must have money." And wealthy relatives desperately searching for you, he considered.

"No." She shook her head thoughtfully. "I was a scholarship student. I remember the day I found out I'd won it. I called Dad up at the station and he came right home and we went out for dinner, at this fancy Beverly Hills restaurant that he couldn't afford."

Sax remained silent, carefully watching her face as she made her way through the stream-of-consciousness account.

"And we ordered champagne and I warned him that he was breaking the law, giving alcohol to a minor and we laughed about what getting arrested would do to his career and he told me not to worry, that he had clout.... He's an L.A. county deputy sheriff," she said with sudden insight.

And that explained her familiarity with his police revolver, Sax decided as another little piece of the puzzle that was Maddy slipped into place.

"Then he undoubtedly has an APB out for you," Sax suggested. "The missing daughter of a county deputy sheriff is bound to garner some attention."

"He probably does," Madeline agreed. She was looking brighter by the minute. "No, wait a minute. He doesn't know I'm missing. Because he's away on his honeymoon."

Sax arched a brow. "Honeymoon?"

"My mother died when I was eighteen," she revealed. "While I was away at school, this widowed real estate lady moved in next door. I watched the romance blossom for years, but her first husband had been an L.A. patrolman who died in the line of duty, so she absolutely refused to marry another cop.

"It was obvious that they were madly in love, but she couldn't take the risk and Dad couldn't imagine being anything else. He also couldn't bring himself to give up the pension he'd worked for so many years to earn. So the affair continued for nearly eight years.

"Then, finally, three weeks after his retirement party, she agreed to get married. They went to her cabin at Lake Arrowhead for the honeymoon." She smiled. "They're both wild about trout fishing."

"Did you go to the wedding?"

"Of course. I wasn't about to miss watching a woman who'd become like a second mother to me become Mrs. Conlan Delaney." Her eyes widened. "Oh! That's my name. Madeline Anne Delaney." She laughed, her voice reminding Sax of sterling-silver wind chimes. "Madeline Anne Delaney." She danced around the room, twirling like a top, her hair flowing out behind her. "Madeline Anne Delaney."

Her smile was bright enough to illuminate not only the darkroom, but the entire Oregon coast, as well. "Isn't that a wonderful, beautiful name?" she asked, stopping in front of him.

Her brandy eyes gleamed with golden flecks he'd never noticed before. Color bloomed in her cheeks, reminding him of the showy rhododendron that grew wild along the coastal highway. Her full lips were parted and so very, very delectable.

"It's a beautiful name," he agreed huskily.

He'd wanted her almost from the beginning. Since such a feeling was not unnatural, especially for a male who'd been without a female for so long, Sax wasn't about to feel guilty for whatever thoughts his hormones might conjure up.

But why hadn't he noticed how breathtakingly lovely this woman was? And how could he not have noticed that the feelings she stirred in him went far deeper than mere need?

"A beautiful name for a beautiful woman."

His eyes lingered on her mouth. He remembered her lightning response to their shared kiss out on the rocks and caught himself wondering if she'd be so warm, so uninhibited, in bed.

Surprising himself yet again, he lifted his hand and caressed her lips with his thumb. "You have a truly remarkable face," he murmured.

He felt her faint grimace beneath his fingertip. "I'll bet you say that to all the bruised and battered women who wash up onto your rocks."

"Only gorgeous amnesiac mermaids who ride in on the backs of whales."

"A dolphin," she managed quietly, her eyes on his. She swallowed. "The whale tipped the boat—it was a dolphin that brought me to shore."

"I stand corrected."

He looked down at her and saw desire, along with a vulnerability that tugged at an unwelcome chord of conscience on her face. Her defenses were low; she was, just as she'd been on the rocks earlier, his for the taking.

Her hair had dried into thick waves that tumbled over her shoulders. Yesterday, when he'd seen her floating facedown in the tidal pool, he'd suspected it would be brown.

Once again it appeared that he'd sorely underestimated her. The tousled waves were the color of autumn leaves—shadings of russet and chestnut, threaded with a dark rich gold.

With the first truly tender gesture he'd given her, he reached out and brushed a wisp of that silken hair from her bruised cheek. He could smell the rain in her hair, the rain and a faint, lingering fragrance that reminded him of a pine forest after a late-summer storm.

His fingers tangled in those tawny waves, tilting her head back. "You're not the only one having problems with your memory, Maddy. Because I've spent most of last night and today trying to remember when I've wanted a woman as much as I want you."

She smiled at that. A slow, infinitely feminine smile designed to beguile the most stalwart of men. Sax realized that if Madeline Anne Delaney chose, she could bring him to his knees; it was not a welcome thought.

"And?" Her rich, throaty voice started a thousand pulses humming just beneath his skin.

He was irritated with himself for being aroused, annoyed with her for arousing him. "I keep coming up blank. And finally, out there on those rocks earlier, I realized why."

She had to ask. "Why?"

"The reason I can't remember ever feeling like this is because I've never—in all my thirty-five years—ever wanted a woman as much as I wanted you then. As much as I still want you at this moment."

Surprise then pleasure flooded into her remarkably open eyes.

Once again the urge to take her now, quickly, fiercely, swept over him like a tidal wave. Would that do it? he wondered agonizingly. If he gave in to the impulses pounding away inside him and made love to this woman, here and now, on the floor of the darkroom, would sanity return? Would he get his life back?

"But it doesn't matter." His fist closed convulsively on her hair. If he had to hurt her to protect her, that's what he would do. If he had to hurt her to save himself, he'd do that, too. "Because I'm not going to take you to bed."

"Oh?" Because of his own inner turmoil, Sax didn't hear the unfamiliar edge to her tone. "I don't understand. I thought you said you wanted me."

"Of course I want you, dammit. But I'm not going to do anything about it."

"Why not?"

"Because it wouldn't be fair to you."

"It wouldn't?"

"No. Because it couldn't lead to anything."

"I see." Her voice was calm. Too calm. But still he failed to notice. "And you take fairness and honesty very seriously, don't you, Sax?"

"I've always tried to."

"So, let me make certain I understand the situation correctly. You want me. And obviously you're man-of-the-world enough to realize that I share those feelings."

"I figured you did." He did not seem thrilled about the knowledge.

"My, the man's perceptive, as well as talented," she murmured. "So, you're attracted to me and I'm attracted to you, but *you're* not going to do anything about it. *You're* not taking me to bed. Because it couldn't lead anywhere."

"That's right." He was relieved she'd grasped his meaning so quickly.

"Don't I have anything to say about any of this?"

His eyes narrowed. "What do you mean?"

"I mean, what makes you think that just because I find you attractive I'd go to bed with you in the first place?"

"Wouldn't you?"

"Maybe." Her admission garnered a smug expression; her fingers almost itched with the urge to slap it off his face. "Maybe not. But if I were to follow my emotions, I certainly wouldn't expect a marriage proposal in the morning, Sax."

"How do you know you're not already married?" he returned as the unpalatable thought suddenly occurred to him. She wasn't wearing a ring, but that didn't prove anything. For all he knew, it could have gotten washed away.

"I'd know," she insisted with instant, unwavering conviction. "I am not married and I know I never have been. But I definitely remember Channing, which proves that I'm not some shy, sheltered little virgin, so you don't have to worry about my police-officer father waiting outside the bedroom door with his service revolver. Or a shotgun."

Pulling her hair free of his hold, she backed away. "You're a difficult man to figure out, Saxon. Every time I think I'm beginning to understand you, I run across another layer. But I never expected to discover that you were a coward."

"A coward?" His tone was calm; his eyes were not. "I'm not a coward."

"Yes, you are," she flared. "You're afraid of your feelings, and I think you've been running from them for a very long time."

As if realizing that he'd revealed more about himself than he'd intended, Sax immediately pulled back. Emotionally and physically. The shutter came back down over his eyes, and his face closed.

"You don't know a damn thing about me."

"I know that you're not as cold or as hard or as unfeeling as you pretend to be. I also know that when I go to bed with a man, I don't want to worry about him waking up with all kinds of recriminations. And I definitely don't want to hear an apology in place of 'good morning.'"

A temper she was rapidly discovering she possessed flared; red flags waved in her cheeks, and her eyes flashed furious sparks. "I do truly appreciate your saving my life, Officer." There was a loud crackling sound. Madeline looked down and saw that the piece of paper she'd forgotten she was holding was crumpled in her fist. "But do me one last favor," she demanded. "Stay away from me until the damn water goes down and I can leave this place and go back to wherever it is I belong!"

No! She belonged here, with him. He'd found her, had breathed his own air into her lungs, pulled her from the dark abyss of death, and although neither of them might be very pleased about their current situation, she was his, dammit.

Sax knew if he actually staked that ridiculous claim out loud, Maddy would think he was certifiable. He also knew, in some distant corner of his mind, that it was exactly what she was waiting to hear.

Even now, even after he'd assured her that he would not take advantage of their situation, of her, Sax's need for her was unreasonable. But the need to hold back proved stronger. Because it had been too long since he'd allowed himself to feel any emotion, and even longer since he'd permitted himself to express any feelings, he didn't say a thing.

"It's suddenly getting crowded in here," she said, frustrated by his coldness. His silence. "I'm going for a walk. Unless you have any objections."

He shrugged. "You're my guest, Madeline. Not my prisoner."

Furious, she flung the crushed ball of paper at his chest, then turned on her heel and marched from the room, slamming the darkroom door behind her.

Sax stared at the door for a full ten seconds, listening to her running down the stairs. A few minutes later, he heard the downstairs door slam, as well.

Muttering a harsh, pungent curse, he closed his eyes, reminded himself that he'd done the right thing—the only possible thing—and returned to the task of making the proofs that might reveal who the hell was responsible for bringing the highly appealing, decidedly frustrating Madeline Anne Delaney into his life.

6

THIS TIME IT WAS SAX who found Madeline standing at the tide pool, staring down at a piece of gray wood that had washed onto shore. The wood bore the letters *Vik*.

"The *Viking Pride*," Sax murmured when she refused to acknowledge his presence. "It's the fishing boat you were on."

A faint memory stirred. "I seem to remember the boat smelling of fish," she agreed. Still she did not look up at him. "I assume you were able to get the name from the photograph."

"Yeah."

The wind was stronger than ever, driving the waves with an even greater force against the rocks, blowing the rain sideways. He came closer, until he was standing directly behind her. Although he wanted to touch her, Sax kept his hands thrust deeply in his pockets to keep them out of trouble.

"So now all we have to do is find out who owned her," Madeline murmured.

Having been furious when she'd left the lighthouse, her mind going around and around like a piece of driftwood in a whirlpool, she had no idea how long she'd been outdoors. Now she began to realize that she was freezing.

Although she told herself that it was only her overactive imagination, stimulated by the events of the past two days, she felt certain that she could feel the warmth radiating from Sax as he stood close—tantalizingly close—behind her.

"That's definitely a start," he agreed. "May I make a suggestion?"

Her only response was an uncaring shrug.

"Come back to the lighthouse with me," Sax coaxed. "It's wet and freezing out here, and although I can understand why you wouldn't want to be under the same roof with such a gruff, uncaring bastard, coming down with pneumonia to spite me would be like cutting off your nose to spite your face."

She tried to keep the soft smile from curving her lips and failed. "My father uses that expression. Whenever he's scolding me for being too stubborn."

"You know what they say," Sax reminded her mildly. "Father knows best."

"That's on television. Not in the real world."

But her father was a wise and caring man, Madeline knew. He also had an uncanny judgment for reading people, which he'd always attributed to sixty percent police experience and forty percent Irish second sight. While growing up under his roof, Madeline had come to trust her father's judgment. And she knew that were he to ever meet Saxon Carstairs, Deputy Sheriff Conlan Delaney would definitely approve.

"Dammit, Sax," she muttered, spinning around to glare up at him. Before she could finish her complaint, her foot slipped on a moss-slick rock.

Sax caught her easily, his hands curved around her shoulders. "You can cuss me out all you want. Once we get out of this storm. Unless you feel like taking another swim."

Her arms came up as if to rest her hands on his shoulders, hesitated, then dropped to her sides again. She could sense that he was on the verge of kissing her once more; worse yet was exactly how badly she wanted him to.

"Has anyone ever told you that you're insufferably bossy?" Madeline asked.

"All the time. And I do my best to live up to the image. Has anyone ever told you that you're incredibly lovely?"

The rain was streaming down her uplifted face. She hadn't worn any makeup for days, and without a blow dryer and a brush to smooth it, her hair was a mass of ungovernable waves. Madeline knew exactly what she looked like. And "lovely" definitely wasn't the word she would have used.

"Even when wet?" she challenged.

Rain pelted them as he ran his fingers down the side of her face. Drops of moisture clung to the thick, tangled lashes surrounding her incredible eyes. "Especially when wet."

The storm swirled like madness around them. Outside, she was freezing. Inside, a warm glow began radiating outward, stimulated by his tender touch. "Dammit, Saxon Carstairs," she complained again, "I really want to hate you."

"Because I'm bossy and overbearing?"

Because you make me feel out of control, she answered silently. *And because I'm not used to feeling that way.* "That, too," she agreed. She gripped her hands together, revealing exactly how hard she was fighting herself. "And because I hate the way you're right all the time." She began to shiver. "It's freezing out here."

"Then you'll come back with me?"

Her chin was angled defiantly, but her voice was breathless. "Do I have any choice?"

"No." His look turned inordinately sober. His eyes were dark and warm and made her heart pound. "To tell you the truth, I don't think either of us has had a choice, mermaid. From the beginning."

Although a little thrill of panic raced through her, there was no way she was going to attempt to answer that intriguing statement while desire was washing over her in enervating waves.

They returned to the lighthouse, hand in hand.

Madeline told herself that the only reason she allowed Sax to hold her hand was to keep her from slipping again on the rain-slick rocks.

Sax told himself that the only reason he didn't want to let go of Madeline's hand was that he wanted to ensure that she didn't slip back into the icy water.

Both knew they were lying. The reason he kept his fingers curled around hers in the seemingly innocent hold, and the reason she kept her hand in his, was that they could no longer be together and not touch.

"Your clothes are soaked again," he commented as they entered the cozy lighthouse.

"I know. You're right, of course—I probably should have stayed indoors, but I was so angry with you . . ." She took a deep breath. "I just had to get away."

"You had every right to be angry," Sax surprised her by saying. "And as much as I hate to admit it, you may be right about me."

This wasn't a man who enjoyed admitting to personal flaws. Knowing how much it took for him to say that, Madeline didn't respond.

"While you were out getting drenched in that storm, I realized that over the past eleven months I've purposely narrowed my entire world to this lighthouse," he said. "To this jetty.

"And then you washed up on my rocks and forced me to face everything I thought I'd given up. Everything I didn't think I'd ever want again."

"Like sex?" It was a difficult question. But she had to know if Sax was attracted to her, or if he was simply responding to her as he might to any available female.

He laughed at that, a rough, gritty laugh that held no humor. "Ah, Maddy. If it were only that simple." He framed her frowning face between his palms. "If all I wanted was a roll in the hay, mermaid, believe me, Satan's Cove is no monastery. For a small town, it definitely has its share of attractive, willing women. Some who have made it quite clear that they wouldn't mind sharing their beds with me."

"How fortunate for you." She hated the jolt of jealousy his answer had instilled.

"Dammit." Sax felt an urge to shake her, an urge he resisted. "Would you just listen to what I'm trying to tell you?"

The stubborn line between her brows, a line he shared on his own face, deepened. But instead of arguing, Madeline exhaled a huff of breath and said, "Go ahead."

Her tone, her straight back, her tilted chin belonged to a deposed Russian duchess; the mass of curly wet hair tumbling over her shoulders and the wide, gold-flecked, whiskey-colored eyes were that of a waif. Sax wondered if the woman had any idea how appealing that striking contrast could be.

"Ever since I got out of the hospital I've been telling myself that I didn't want to care about anyone. Ever again. It's not that I'm selfish, because I don't think I am. It's just that I was all used up. Can you understand that?"

Having witnessed a few of her father's close friends suffering from police burn-out, Madeline nodded. "Yes," she said softly. "I think I can."

"So I came here," he continued. "Where I could be alone and where I'd never have to be put in the position of having to do anything for anyone. Where I'd never be responsible for anyone."

"And then I showed up and ruined your carefully laid plans."

"Blew them all right out of the water," he agreed gruffly.

Sax felt his heart softening as he gazed down into her face. Her eyes were wide and reflected both misgiving and hope. He found the combination impossible to resist. He'd always prided himself on the ability to remain ice cool under pressure. Saxon Carstairs's reputation, both professionally and personally, had always been one of unwavering logic and deliberate action. But now, against all reason, against his not inconsiderable will, he found himself growing closer and closer to a woman who elicited pure emotion.

Unfortunately he'd already determined that this was a woman deserving of an emotional commitment he was not prepared to make.

"I'm finding it more and more difficult not to care for you, Madeline Delaney. And I'm finding it impossible not to want to protect you." His gaze skimmed over her so quickly his eyes barely left hers. "Which right now means getting you out of those wet clothes." Not wanting her to misunderstand his meaning, he quickly tacked on, "There's a woman's sweat suit hanging in my closet. Why don't you change while I heat up some lunch?"

He'd let his guard down just long enough for Madeline to get a glimpse inside, at the Saxon Carstairs who was still suffering from the loss of his partner, a loss she suspected he held himself somehow responsible for. She'd also seen a man who had once believed in so much. And now, because of a cruel twist of fate, Sax believed in nothing. Not even, she considered sadly, himself.

"I don't think I'd be comfortable wearing someone else's clothes." The truth was that she hated discovering that some other woman had been close enough to Sax during these months of self-imposed exile to keep a change of clothing in his isolated lighthouse.

"They don't actually belong to another woman. They're my wife's."

"Wife?" Dear Lord, she'd never even considered the fact that Sax might be married. To lust after a complete stranger was bad enough; to lust after a married man was a completely different and much more serious kettle of fish.

Years of Catholic school had left their imprint on Madeline's strict moral code; she had a sudden urge to glance down and see if a scarlet *A* had suddenly appeared on the front of her sweater.

"Ex-wife," Sax corrected. "We've been divorced for almost six years."

Her quick feeling of relief was immediately transcended by the unpalatable thought that even though they'd been divorced for all those years, Sax's former wife's clothes were upstairs hanging in his closet. A closet he'd only had for less than a year. Cozy, Madeline considered grimly.

"It must have been a very friendly divorce." Her cool tone was calculated to conceal both her unwilling attraction for Sax and the vulnerability that went with it.

Sax heard the edge in her tone, wondered if she could be jealous of Ellen and decided that he was jumping to conclusions. "Actually it was. We were impossibly mismatched and fought like tigers when we were married, but as soon as we signed the papers, we were best friends again."

"How nice for you."

This time it would have been impossible to miss the acid of resentment in her voice. Even as he reminded himself that he'd vowed not to get emotionally involved with this woman, Sax decided that he rather liked the idea that Maddy was actually jealous of his former wife.

"When I met Ellen, she was running an art gallery in San Francisco," he told her. "It was a small, trendy little shop in Cow Hollow, dealing mostly in photographic art. After we got married, she moved to Portland and started using her contacts with the West Coast art community to act as an artist's representative.

"She's my agent, Maddy. Our relationship is strictly professional."

"Oh." She tried for a tone of absolute disinterest and failed. "Well, it's nice that you have someone you can trust handling your business affairs."

"Yes. It is."

It was obvious that she cared. Just as it was becoming more and more obvious that he and Madeline were sitting atop a powder keg. Despite his best intentions, their mutual attraction had lit the fuse; now the question was no longer *if* the damn thing was going to blow sky-high, but *when*.

"I don't know much about women's sizes, but I think the outfit should fit you."

Although he'd come to the conclusion that Maddy was a living, breathing example of that old axiom about the best things coming in small packages, he decided that she probably wouldn't appreciate his mentioning that his former wife was a great deal more curvaceous.

Madeline felt him back away again, physically and emotionally. It was just as well, she decided. Because she needed time. Time to try to understand what was happening to her. Time to figure out what she was going to do. Not just about whatever trouble she'd been in before she landed here on Sax's jetty, but these confusing, perilous feelings she'd been experiencing toward the man.

Although she knew he'd never physically harm her, he frightened her just the same. What was even more frightening was how she was fast discovering that certain kinds of fear could be exhilarating.

THE SWEAT SUIT HAD BEEN created from a lush, dark purple velour trimmed in gold braid. A gold-embossed emblem adorned the breast, and the label revealed it to be from Neiman Marcus. That no one had ever actually sweated in such luxurious loungewear was obvious.

Standing in front of the mirror, turning this way and that, observing the unfamiliar woman reflected in the glass, Madeline felt like an imposter. Leaning closer, she rubbed at the line between her tawny brows with her fingertip. Madeline sighed at the slender woman with the angular face, too-wide eyes, pointed chin and unruly hair that was neither brown nor red nor dark blond, but an undisciplined blending of all three.

The woman who would normally wear this outfit would be chic and blond and smell of Giorgio or Obsession. Her jewelry would be twenty-four-karat gold, her diamonds would be of exceptional blue-white clarity. She'd be self-assured and rather than walking, she would glide, like a Paris runway model. She would be, Madeline decided, a woman trained from birth to be an intelligent, attractive foil to an equally successful man.

Madeline tried to imagine Sax of the faded jeans and worn sweatshirt being married to a woman who would wear such expensive clothing but couldn't. Once again she realized that there were far more layers to the enigmatic, arrogant, self-contained man than met the eye.

She told herself that she didn't want to understand him. She reminded herself that her biggest problem right now was to figure out who it was who'd tried to kill her. And why.

But as she entered the kitchen and was greeted by a welcoming smile, her resolve to keep her emotional distance from this man melted away like a sand castle at high tide.

"It fits," Sax said.

"Sort of." She'd had to roll both the pants and the sleeves up. "Your wife—ex-wife," she corrected firmly, "must be tall."

"I suppose she is. Now that you mention it." He had to repress his smile. She looked like a little girl playing dress-up in her mother's clothes; he much preferred the sweater and snug jeans. "Tell you what. I'll put your stuff in the dryer after we finish lunch. It shouldn't take that long to dry."

"Thanks." She looked down at the lush purple material. "I don't think this is really me."

"Thank God for that," Sax murmured beneath his breath, but loud enough that Madeline heard him all the same.

She couldn't keep the smile from blooming on her lips at the knowledge that perhaps his relationship with his former wife wasn't as intimate as she'd supposed.

"I hope you like seafood."

"I love it."

"Good. Because I heated up some bouillabaisse." He put two steaming bowls filled with a variety of clams and mussels in a dark red sauce on the table, followed by a loaf of crusty French bread. "I thought it might take the chill off."

Actually, as he'd worked downstairs, imagining her stripping off that wet clothing on the floor above, Sax had thought of a lot more appealing ways to warm his mermaid up—several of them dealing with his ancient bathtub—but had reluctantly decided to stick with the fish stew.

She sat down in the chair he held out for her. "That's very considerate of you," she murmured absently. Unruly thoughts of making love to Sax in his old-fashioned bathtub were flashing through her mind. Now that would be the way to take the chill off, Madeline mused.

"I told you—"

"I know." She took the paper napkin from beside the bowl and placed it on her lap. "You're never considerate. You also lied because, although you don't want to admit it, you're one of the most thoughtful men I've ever known."

Sax sat across from her. "That's not saying very much, since you can't remember all the other men you've known."

She smiled. "I can remember enough," she corrected mildly. "You'd be surprised how much is coming back to me."

He found himself wondering if she had a current lover and decided not to ask. Although experience had taught him that ignorance was seldom bliss, sometimes it could be convenient.

"I've been thinking," he said as he poured two glasses of wine from a dark green bottle. "Given what you said about attending Northwestern's school of journalism, and that summer workshop in Santa Barbara, it's probable that you're a journalist."

"I came to the same conclusion," Madeline agreed. "While I was walking out along the rocks." She took a sip of the rosy burgundy and found it smooth and light and a perfect counterpart to the hearty stew.

"It's also likely that you were working on a story that got you in hot water. Or in this case, cold water."

She smiled at him over the rim of her glass. "What do you know, it's true—great minds really do think alike."

He returned the smile, enjoying her company. Enjoying her. "I don't suppose you'd happen to recall what story you were chasing down."

"No." She put her glass down and rubbed her temples. Her headache was coming back again. With a vengeance.

Sax observed the telling gesture and knew it was better not to push. Reaching across the table, he took her hand in his. "Hey, in case you've forgotten, you've had a traumatic twenty-four hours. You were almost killed, you almost drowned. A few hours ago, you didn't even remember your name." His thumb brushed over her knuckles. "You've made remarkable progress, Madeline."

"Not enough."

"Give it time," he counseled again. "You can't do anything until the storm moves on and the water goes down, anyway. In the meantime, you're perfectly safe here with me."

The afternoon light had dimmed to deep purple, creating vague, unearthly shadows on the cream-colored walls and oak-plank floor. Fog curled around the towering white building, clinging to the windows like smoke, making the interior of the kitchen seem to shrink. Outside, the wind wailed, and thunder rumbled over the sea.

His fingers tightened around hers as their eyes met and held. Madeline had never been so aware of a man; she'd never been so aware of herself. There was a tug-of-war going on inside her, battering away at her with more intensity than yesterday's icy waves.

Sax told himself that he had no business losing his head over any woman, let alone one who'd soon be out of his life. He'd just gotten himself caught up in her admittedly intriguing problems. That was all it was. That was all he would allow it to be.

Uninvited, the storm had moved inside the light-house, and in that suspended moment, both Madeline and Sax silently acknowledged that until it passed, neither of them was safe.

THE TWO MEN—one gray and elegant, the other dark and dangerous—met at a deserted warehouse in the waterfront district. Although it was risky for them to meet face-to-face like this, he had reluctantly come to the conclusion that there was far more risk in not meeting at all.

He didn't want to receive this information second-hand. He didn't want to give such a vital assignment by proxy. He wanted to watch the man's face as he told what he knew; he needed to see his reaction when he told him what must be done.

"Pieces of the boat have washed up on the shore," the man who was already waiting for him offered without preamble.

"Where?"

When the man hesitated, he cursed silently and pulled an envelope from the breast pocket of his cashmere trench coat. That was the trouble with the world today; everyone had gotten so damn greedy.

Somewhere in the distance, out on the mighty Columbia River, a foghorn sounded; the sound of sea gulls fighting for scraps echoed on the foggy air.

The man stuck the envelope into his own pocket without opening it. "Satan's Cove."

He exhaled a relieved breath. The knot in his stomach loosened slightly for the first time in days. "Then it shouldn't be that difficult to find out what happened to the woman. The town only has, what, two hundred inhabitants?"

"One hundred and thirty-five."

He nodded, pleased. He'd been told this was a man who did his homework; obviously his information had been correct. "Has she been seen?"

"Not yet. But I've got people working on it."

"That's not good enough." The knot in his gut tugged again. "I want you to handle this personally."

The man registered not a glimmer of surprise. "That'll cost extra."

Nerves twisted. He waved a leather-gloved hand with far more calm than he was feeling. "I'm prepared to pay whatever it costs."

Although he knew it was highway robbery, he managed not to flinch at the price the man quoted. Life had taught him that you got what you paid for. Some things—and some people—did not come cheap.

"I don't want to meet again until this is all over," he said. "It's too damn dangerous." The idea of what he was prepared to do wasn't nearly as disturbing as he might have expected; the thought of getting caught was terrifying.

"Hey, it's your call." As if he'd been expecting such an answer, the dark man handed over a small piece of paper. "You can deposit the money directly into my Bahamian account. Half now, the other half when the job's completed.

"As soon as I'm told the money's in the bank, I'll go to Satan's Cove. If the woman's alive, I'll find her."

"And if she's dead?"

"I'll still find her."

He had no doubt that the man was telling the truth. He had, after all, come highly recommended. "There's something else."

The man's eyes remained as hard and flat as stones; his only expression was a slight twisting of the upper lip that could have been the beginnings of a smile. Or a smirk.

"I thought there might be."

"If you find the woman..." He hesitated and glanced around the deserted building as if looking for spies. "And somehow she managed to survive..." He paused again.

"I'll kill her," the man supplied without blinking an eye. The actual purpose for this meeting finally out in the open, the hired assassin proceeded to name his price as easily as if he were discussing the weather.

He nodded, relieved not to have had to say the words himself. Paying to rid himself of a vexatious problem was one thing; he'd managed, with remarkable ease, to convince himself that it was not that different from hiring an exterminator to rid a warehouse of mice.

But actually saying the words would somehow have brought him down to this man's level. And that idea grated more than the possibility of murder itself.

"I'm pleased to see we understand each other."

The man's derisive laugh startled a rat, sending it scurrying across the concrete floor. "Absolutely."

7

THE STORM RAGED for another three days. On the first day, after Sax's less-than-enthusiastic admission concerning his desire for Madeline, by mutual, unspoken consent, they tried to maintain an emotional and physical distance from each other. But since the lighthouse was far from spacious, the strained effort proved exhausting.

"This is ridiculous," Sax complained the following morning.

Madeline glanced up from spreading marmalade on her toast. The dark shadows beneath his stormy eyes revealed that he hadn't gotten any more sleep downstairs on the couch than she had upstairs, alone in that too-wide bed.

"Excuse me?" she asked politely.

"Trying to establish the Grand Canyon between us," Sax elaborated. "It isn't working and we're both miserable, and this place is too damn small to keep out of each other's way. We're not teenagers, Maddy. So why don't we just agree to keep our hormones under control and make the best of the situation."

"I'm not the one who spent all day yesterday glowering," she noted calmly.

"Dammit, I wasn't glowering." Sax slammed his mug onto the table. Coffee sloshed over the rim and went ignored.

"Oh, you've been a model of congeniality," she agreed.

He gave her a sharp glance. Then slowly his expression softened. "Anyone ever tell you that you have a smart mouth?"

She smiled serenely. "Sorry. I don't recall."

"Convenient memory you have there, mermaid."

"Isn't it?"

He drew in a rough, ragged breath. "All right," he admitted reluctantly, "perhaps I haven't been exactly hospitable. But I'm willing to compromise."

Madeline braced her elbows on the table, rested her chin on her linked fingers and waited.

"Since you seem to know your way around a darkroom, and since we're stuck on this jetty until the storm passes, we may as well see if we can work together."

"Are you offering me a job?"

"No. I'm simply saying that if you'd like to keep me company while I work, I wouldn't mind."

It was, Madeline decided, the closest he could come to asking for her companionship. And while it wasn't much, it was a beginning. Besides, yesterday she'd begun to go out of her mind, left all alone in the lighthouse while he'd walked along the shore in the morning and spent the afternoon and evening hidden away in his darkroom.

"I'd like that," she said.

A ghost of a smile teased at the corners of his lips. Sax controlled it. "Fine," he agreed. "We'll give it a try and see how it goes."

It went better than either of them could have expected. Sax quickly determined that Maddy had a unique way of looking at things, seeing art in commonplace items that he might have ignored. Always before, his artistic vision had gone for the bold and the strong: vast landscapes, roiling waves, pods of playful whales.

But as they braved the inclement weather, canvasing the shoreline for photo opportunities, Madeline showed him that he could narrow his focus considerably and still end up with something special. Something as unique as the woman herself.

A lone piece of driftwood, stranded on a narrow strip of wet gray sand, became a silvery modern sculpture; a scattering of shells left behind by the ebbing tide was turned into a delicate montage of shapes and shadows. Even glistening sea foam became new when seen through her wide, eager eyes.

Not that he abandoned his usual vision. As she worked beside him in the darkroom, watching the photographs take shape, Madeline realized that Sax had managed to capture the fury and intensity of the sea perfectly.

Which made sense, she decided. Obviously Sax could identify with the dark and dangerous weather raging against the windswept coast since it was more than a little obvious that he had his own storm battering away inside him. The same storm that was playing havoc with her own emotions. Because, try as they might, as the days passed and they grew inevitably closer, they were finding it more and more difficult to keep desire at bay.

"You know," she said one evening over a dinner of salmon steaks and new potatoes, "I had a thought today." It was the fifth day of her stay in the lighthouse.

So had he. When she'd reached in front of him for a roll of film, her hair had brushed against his cheek. He'd inhaled its forest scent, and it had demanded a major effort not to take her beneath the unworldly glow of the amber light.

"Have you remembered something else?" He refilled her glass with white wine.

The return of her memory, which in the beginning had seemed so promising, was definitely stalled. Although Madeline could recall bits and pieces of her former life—most particularly little intimate, unimportant incidents—try as she might, she could not remember what had brought her to Oregon. And what story she'd been working on that had led her into such perilous waters.

The harder she attempted to remember, the more barriers she encountered. And her escalating feelings for Sax were no help. Their situation was creating a maelstrom of stress, and the more stressful Madeline felt, the more mental barricades popped up, impeding the return of her memory.

"No." Madeline took a sip of wine and tried not to feel discouraged.

"It'll come," he told her for the umpteenth time. "The trick is—"

"Not to push it. I know." She ran her fingers up and down the stem of the heavy crystal glass and attempted to choose her words carefully. "I was thinking about you."

Sax eyed her cautiously over the rim of his own glass. "About me?"

"About your work."

"Oh."

She watched him visibly relax. It was obvious that he was still uncomfortable discussing anything personal. "I was thinking," she suggested slowly, "that you should do a book."

"I'm a photographer, not a writer."

"A book of photographs."

"One of those big coffee-table things that come out every year just in time for Christmas?"

"Exactly." She took another drink of wine. *Liquid courage*, she could hear her father scolding. "Your photographs are marvelous, Sax. And graphic books are in great demand, not to mention the fact that the Northwest is an 'in' location right now because of the environmental movement."

He rubbed his jaw thoughtfully as he considered her words. "I don't know, Maddy. I'm just getting started. I don't know if I want to start thinking about books and publishing houses and all that stuff."

"It doesn't matter how long you've been a professional," she argued. "What matters is that you're good. You could call it the *Sunset Coast*."

"A book would require text," he returned. "And I'm not a writer."

"I am."

There was a long, drawn-out silence. Finally Sax said, "I don't think I'm ready, Maddy."

Was he not ready to create a book? she wondered. Or, more likely, not ready to consider a future with her in it? Madeline let out a breath she'd been unaware of holding. "It was just a thought."

Seeing the disappointment in her eyes and feeling like a heel for being the bastard to put it there, Sax reached across the table and covered her hand with his. "It was a good thought, mermaid. Just a little premature."

The conversation concluded, albeit unsatisfactorily, they returned their attention to their dinner. But the flaky Alaskan salmon had turned to ashes in Madeline's mouth, and she was relieved when the excruciatingly long meal finally came to an end.

After they'd done the dishes in silence, Sax said he was going to put in a few more hours of work before turning in. He didn't invite Madeline to join him, and she didn't offer.

Instead, she went upstairs to the bedroom he'd turned over to her, crawled beneath the covers and pretended to read. But as hard as she tried to keep her mind on the words, all her thoughts were directed upstairs. Toward Sax.

Their dilemma was increasingly frustrating. As much as she wanted to stick to their agreement, Madeline felt as if every nerve ending in her body was on the verge of screaming.

She was not alone.

Upstairs, as he worked alone in the dark, developing the photographs that he knew were his best work to date, the hunger raging inside Sax had built to monumental proportions. He wanted Maddy with a desperation he'd never felt before; unwilling to give in to the temptation he knew they were both feeling, he threw himself into his work. All his frustration, all his tumultuous emotions—emotions that rivaled the storm he was capturing on film—were revealed in the photographs he was developing every afternoon. The storm outside escalated with the same intensity as the tempest inside him. And it showed on every print.

During these past days, when he'd forced himself to keep his distance from Madeline, Sax had come to the unwelcome realization that his hunger did not come from the fact that he'd been eighteen months without a woman. No, these feelings that had been tormenting him from that first night she'd slept so restlessly atop him had nothing to do with that. They came from the woman herself; they were born of his overwhelming need for this one very special woman. And that was precisely what made them so dangerous.

Downstairs Madeline was unbearably restless, plagued with dreams and desires and frustrations. She paced the floor of the bedroom long into the night, wondering if Sax was still awake. Wondering if he was thinking of her.

He was.

He lay on the too-short couch, listening to her pace the floor and realized once again that she was every bit as restless as he. It would be so easy, he told himself. All he'd have to do would be to climb those stairs, strip off whatever clothing she might be wearing, kiss her lips long and hard and deep, and she would be his for the taking.

Sax had never thought of himself as a fanciful man. But as the pendulum clock struck two o'clock in the morning, he allowed his fantasies to take flight. He imagined what it would be like to make love to Maddy Delaney, imagined tasting her golden skin—her throat, her shoulders, her pert little breasts. He pictured himself drawing slow, aching circles over that firm, supple flesh; he could practically hear her soft sighs, her throaty moans.

Slowly, drawing out both the pleasure and the pain, his lips would follow the trail his hands had blazed, and then her rosy nipple would be between his lips like a ripe berry, and as he licked on the sensitive flesh, he would feel it becoming hard and erect as she grew more and more excited.

As his mental images became more and more vivid and erotic, his body throbbed with unrequited need. It was torture; if he insisted on continuing, he might as well go somewhere they practiced self-flagellation, because the mood he was in tonight, he'd definitely fit right in.

The aching deepened as he imagined slipping between her silken thighs, entering the welcoming warmth of her body with a single thrust. Their lovemaking would be slow and sensual and go on and on until finally, hours later, they would both be too exhausted and too satiated to move.

"Dammit." Sax groaned and, shifting painfully on the couch, adjusted the cotton briefs that were suddenly too tight for comfort. Glaring out into the well of darkness outside the window, he willed the storm to stop. Because if he had to spend one more celibate night under the same roof with his siren, he'd go mad.

THEY WERE GOING to kill her.

The thought flashed through Madeline's mind, as vivid and deadly as the lightning forking across the storm black sky.

The boat rocked on the churning waves that were cresting at fifteen feet; a clap of thunder directly overhead rocked the boat; a flash of lightning illuminated the pitching sea. The boat rose and fell, plummeting down the back of a huge swell. Spray hit against the sides of the cabin with the sound of flying gravel.

Closing her eyes, Madeline dived headfirst into the whitecapped maelstrom. The churning black tide swallowed her up, covering her like a shroud.

HER SCREAMS WOKE HIM from a restless sleep. Taking the stairs two at a time, Sax burst into the room. His heart, pounding painfully in his chest, skipped a beat when he saw that the bed was empty.

His gaze swept around the room, and he saw her standing in a corner, her arms wrapped around herself. Outside the window, the storm had finally passed, leaving behind diamond bright stars glittering in a sky of black velvet. Moonlight streamed into the room; in the shimmering silvery dust Sax could see her eyes, wide, unseeing and terrified.

"It's all right, Maddy," he crooned. Although he wanted to go to her, he remained beside the bed, afraid that too quick a movement would only frighten her more. "You're safe. Here in the lighthouse. With me."

She dragged a trembling hand through her sleep-tousled hair; recognition slowly began to dawn in her eyes. "Sax?"

It was only a ragged whisper, but Sax thought he'd never heard his name sound so sweet. "It's me, sweetheart," he assured her. The need to go to her was so strong, he had to curl his left hand into a fist and hold on to the bedpost with his right to keep from acting on impulse.

She had commandeered one of his T-shirts. The ash gray shirt with the black letters PPD, which stood for Portland Police Department, covered her from her shoulders to her knees. She looked small and vulnerable. And, Sax considered, remembering his fantasy with vivid accuracy, damn sexy.

"I was so afraid." She pressed a hand against her breast, as if to quiet her pounding heart. "I was on the boat, and it was raining and then I was drowning."

"You were dreaming." Still concerned about re-stimulating her fear, he forced himself to remain where he was. "It was only a nightmare." He held out his hand. "It's okay."

She bit her lip and eyed him fearfully. Her frightened gaze circled the room. Then, as he watched, things clicked into place. "Oh, Sax." Her knees buckled with belated relief. Lunging forward, Sax caught her just before she crumpled to the floor.

"It's all right, Maddy," he said against her hair. He held her tightly against him, his hands moving over her as if to assure her that she was really there, with him. Whole and safe.

His chest was firm against her cheek; his arms were wrapped protectively around her. As she felt the heat of his touch burning through the cotton T-shirt, Madeline's heart was still thudding. But not with fear. She leaned against him, eyes closed, absorbing his strength, his warmth.

"It seemed so real."

"I know." He stroked her back, his touch meant to comfort, not arouse. But it did.

All the reasons why this was a mistake fled her mind. She forgot all her vows not to get emotionally involved with Sax, all the rules—spoken and unspoken—that they'd established to keep the inevitable from happening.

Sax knew that if he was going to stop this, the time to move away was now. If he wanted to prevent himself from falling headlong into a relationship he hadn't asked for, hadn't wanted, all he had to do was to leave. Now.

A very strong part of him wanted to walk away, to prove that he still could. He didn't. Because whatever was happening to him, to his mind, his body, his heart, was beyond his power to stop. So, instead of retreating, as he had for days, he stayed where he was; his hands moved to her waist to draw her even closer. He felt her heart beat, heard her soft breath tremble out between her lips.

Reasons no longer mattered. Vows were forgotten. Consequences were ignored. He wanted. She wanted. And for now, that was all that was important.

Madeline tilted her head back, and her eyes met his warmly. There was no need for words; her rich look said everything there was to say.

Sax curved his long fingers around the back of her neck tenderly.

A knowing smile touched Madeline's lips softly.

Lowering his head, Sax kissed her lingeringly.

The kiss began as a mere brushing of lips, a gentle, feather-light pressure that was a prelude, more promise than proper kiss. His lips were cool and firm, hers were soft and warm.

Sax had never met a woman whose emotions simmered so closely beneath the surface. He kissed her slowly, tantalizingly, and felt her quick response. He kissed her gently, patiently, and felt as if he were slowly killing himself.

Struggling valiantly for control, he dragged his lips from hers, pressed his mouth against her throat and felt her pulse flutter. Hauling in a deep, painful breath, he fought the need to take her quickly, fiercely.

He hadn't wanted the responsibility of a woman who needed his protection, but he wanted Maddy. He'd never wanted the restrictions of a home or a family. But he wanted her.

"I've been going out of my mind, spending every night downstairs, knowing that you were sleeping in my bed, that your arms were wrapped around my pillow when they should have been wrapped around me." Impatient, hungry, Sax dragged his mouth back to hers and kissed her, slowly, deeply, using his lips, his teeth, his tongue, until she was limp in his arms. Her lips were warm, heady and unbearably sweet. He could have kissed her endlessly.

And still he wanted more.

"Do you have any idea how it feels to be slowly driven mad?" he asked against her softly parted lips after they'd finally come up for air.

"Yes," she managed on a ragged whisper. She barely realized where she was; she was unaware that her nails were digging into his bare shoulders. She only knew that for that golden suspended time, as the kiss had gone on and on and on, the entire world had centered on the heat and the taste of his lips. "I know." Because she'd been going crazy herself, alone in his wide bed, with only wishes and dreams to keep her company.

His teeth closed over her earlobe; his hands slid beneath the T-shirt to stroke the smoothness of her body, exploring, possessing. "Tell me you want me," he demanded.

"Of course I want you," she answered shakily. She pressed her palm against his cheek and felt the muscle jerk beneath her fingertips. "I've wanted you for days. Forever."

She heard him murmur—it could have been an oath or a prayer—as he dragged her closer.

She was soft, but she was far from safe. He wanted her—too much for comfort, too much for sanity. But like a man beguiled by a mythical siren, as he buried his face in her thick hair, Sax allowed himself to be bewitched.

Although he'd always considered himself a generous lover, the time had passed for slow, leisurely loving. Hunger too long suppressed exploded, catapulting them into a dark, swirling maelstrom where passion ruled and sanity disintegrated.

Sax's control snapped, and then, as if in a chain reaction, Maddy's followed. For now, only this heady, seductive present mattered. Yesterday was forgotten; tomorrow would be ignored.

Racked by the building storm of emotions, they fell to the bed, lips fused, hearts pounding jackhammer swift, jackhammer hard. Greedy and impatient, he yanked the T-shirt over her head and flung it carelessly across the room; with equal frenzy, without taking her mouth from his, Madeline stripped him of his cotton briefs.

And then finally they were naked. Her firm breasts pushed against his chest; the subtle curves made him ache. Her thick hair tumbled over his face and made him burn.

How many times in the past five days had he imagined her like this? How many times had he imagined them coming together this way, breathless and urgent in a torrent of need? Too many to count. A dark and dangerous passion swirled around them, lighter than air, heavier than the sea.

His mouth rushed hungrily over her face; his hands moved heatedly over her skin, discovering points of pain and pleasure that she'd never known existed. Although he'd wanted to be tender, had always planned to be gentle, it seemed he had no gentleness to give her.

But Madeline didn't seem to want gentleness. Indeed, her own hands were far from idle, racing over his own taut body, stroking, exploring, causing jolts of pleasure to shoot through him.

It was as if the laws of gravity had been suspended; they moved freely, effortlessly, as if they'd been taken fathoms beneath the sea, their lovemaking awash in liquid pleasure.

Like a drowning man, he clung to her as he was pulled into the depths. Dragging his mouth from hers, Sax planted kisses, passionate, hot kisses, all over her fluid body. Her flesh—those angry, bluish black bruises now faded to a yellowish hue—bloomed beneath his lips, her breathing seemed to echo in the hot dark room, and she turned effortlessly in his arms, welcoming everything he did to her.

Madeline struggled to fill her lungs with air. She was drowning in needs she'd never before experienced, needs she could not understand. "Sax, please." Her hands fretted down his back, then lower, drawing him against her.

His own breath was coming in pants as he stroked the inside of her thighs. Her warm flesh was as soft and slick as satin. His fingers combed through the nest of soft, curly hair; his hand closed possessively over her pulsating core.

She breathed his name on a sob, a cry, writhing against his palm, clinging to him.

Covering her mouth with his, he slipped one dark, wicked finger inside her.

She was so hot. So moist. So ready.

"You're mine, Maddy." When his thumb caressed the ultrasensitive little nub, she gave a little moan of surrender. Her eyes, shimmering with need and some other, more dangerous emotion that he dare not dwell upon, gave him his answer. But Sax wanted more.

"Tell me." With clever hands and treacherous lips he teased rather than possessed, aroused rather than fulfilled. "I want to hear you say the words."

But Madeline was beyond words. Beyond reason. "Yours," she managed. The single word reverberated in her head, but her soft, husky breath was barely audible. Swallowing painfully, she tried again. "I'm yours, Sax."

His uncharacteristic, fierce need for possession disturbed him. But her ragged response succeeded in shaking him to the core.

And then his body took over, keeping him from dwelling on these puzzling, atypical feelings. Unable to hold back another minute, Sax plunged into her with a force that left them equally stunned and breathless.

There was a sound like the roar of the surf inside his head; she gripped him tightly, as if he were an anchor in a dangerous sea.

Sax paused to give her body time to grow accustomed to the erotic invasion, to give her time to adjust to him. And then he began to move with a deep, rhythmic stroke that echoed the age-old force of the surf pounding against the rocks outside the lighthouse.

Legs tangled, arms tight, together they rode the cresting waves of passion, giving completely to each other, holding nothing back.

All the time, Sax never took his eyes from her face. He watched her eyes darken then cloud as he drove her higher and higher; he watched them widen as he took her up the first high, tumultuous crest. And he watched her lips part in surprise and stunned pleasure as she went crashing over the other side.

Then he gave himself up to the hot, tumultuous waves of ecstasy.

HAD HOURS PASSED? Days? An eternity? Sax lay in the dark, breathless and dazed, struggling to clear his mind. What had happened to him? What demon had taken control of his mutinous body and made him take her so quickly, treat her so roughly?

He was thirty-five years old; he'd lost his virginity eighteen years ago on a senior high school ski trip to Mount Hood. He and Kathi Olson had both been nervous but eager virgins; they'd fumbled unsatisfactorily through the motions that first time, but by the time they'd graduated and gone their separate ways six months later, they'd learned a great deal.

Over the years, he'd gained more experience. Enough that he was able to demonstrate control in such situations, enough that several women had praised him afterward for his finesse.

He'd thought he'd experienced passion before; he believed he'd known pain. He'd been wrong on both counts.

Madeline didn't move; she didn't speak. Her arms were no longer around him, but had slipped to her sides. She lay there, limp, with her eyes closed, her lashes a lush fringe against her still-flushed cheeks, her deep, uneven breaths the only clue that she hadn't fallen asleep.

Bracing himself on one elbow, he looked down at her. Moonlight streamed its silvery dust over her body, making her love-moistened flesh gleam like pearls. Frowning, Sax viewed the new bruises darkening her skin; bruises that hadn't been there the night he'd pulled her from the sea.

Swearing, he reached out and tentatively touched one darkening mark on her thigh that, he remembered with a flash of dark guilt, had been made by his teeth.

As if reading his mind, Madeline slowly opened her eyes. "If you even dare try to apologize, I'm going to toss you out of this bed."

"I hurt you."

Regret was clawing away at his insides. He touched her face and was surprised to find it wet. No wonder she was crying, he considered. After the way he'd treated her.

She surprised him by smiling. A slow, sensual smile that was at direct odds with her tears but spoke volumes just the same. "Just wait until you see your back," she advised mildly. "You won't be able to take your shirt off in public for weeks."

He brushed the moisture away with the back of his hand, horrified by the way his fingers trembled. "You're crying."

"Not because you hurt me." She captured his wrist and brought his fingertips to her lips, kissing them one at a time. "Men are such idiots," she murmured. "It's a wonder why we women put up with you."

"Beats me," he said, struggling to keep his voice steady as his body began to burn all over again.

Still smiling, she kissed his lips once, lightly, then her mouth began skimming down his throat. "I suppose it's because of the sex. You do manage to do that very well."

When her mouth got to the jagged line bisecting his chest, the scar that was a mute reminder of everything he'd wanted to put behind him, she lifted her eyes to his. Sax waited for her to say something and was relieved when she didn't.

She pressed soft, damp kisses against the angry red flesh, then moved on. "Speaking of sex . . ." she murmured as her lips continued their slow, torturous assault of his body.

"Maddy . . ."

"Shh." Her breath was a hot breeze against his stomach. When she probed delicately at his navel with the tip of her tongue, Sax sucked in a harsh breath. "Just let me touch you, Sax," she breathed silkily. "Let me make love to you for a little while more."

Sax closed his eyes and managed, with a herculean effort, to locate the control he'd lost earlier. Her lips roamed down his body in a sensual quest; she seemed determined to discover all his weaknesses, including ones he'd never known he possessed. He did his best to oblige her request. But a few more inches, then he was utterly lost.

This time they made love leisurely, with tenderness and a mutual desire to please. They tasted, they touched, and they loved.

Afterward they lay together, floating on a sea of tranquillity. Her head was nestled on his shoulder, and his arms were wrapped around her. Basking in the cooling aftermath of passion, neither Sax nor Madeline said anything for a long, comfortable time.

Her hair was spread over her, over him, like a tawny curtain.

"Your hair smells like a rain forest."

"It's your shampoo," she murmured.

He grabbed a handful of the tawny waves and lifted it to his lips. "Ah, but it smells a lot better on you."

She smiled, gave a long, luxurious sigh and nestled even closer. Her eyes were closed, her body limp. It was the first time he'd seen her utterly, thoroughly relaxed, and Sax allowed himself a moment's masculine pride for having brought her such absolute contentment.

Although she still didn't know what she was doing here in Oregon, Madeline was certain of one important truth—she'd come home. She knew, with a deepseated instinct that went all the way to the bone, that she'd never felt this way about any other man.

"Sax?"

"Hmm?" He ran his hand down her moist flesh, from her shoulder to her thigh, enjoying the way he could make her tremble even now. Even after all they'd shared.

"I think I'm falling in love with you."

Madeline had not planned to say the words. But now that she had, she didn't want to take them back. There were already so many secrets between them. So many secrets about his life that he would not tell her, so many secrets about her life that she could not tell him. She wanted this truth, at least, to be out in the open.

"Maddy..."

She felt him retreat from her, although he didn't move.

The tide of passion had receded; the soft, floating pleasure faded away, leaving her very much alone on a barren shore. Madeline sighed and schooled her expression to a calm acceptance she was a very long way from feeling. "I don't expect you to love me back, Sax," she said, pressing her fingers against his lips.

The truth she saw in his eyes, as unpalatable as it might be, she could handle. But Madeline didn't think she could bear hearing a lie—no matter how well-meaning—come from his harshly cut lips. Lips she could still taste, even now.

He'd hurt her, dammit. Sax saw the pain in her eyes, pain she was trying valiantly to hide. She'd proved herself so brave, so gutsy, that he'd forgotten the little fact that she'd be bound to think like a woman.

What to him had been a straightforward, fundamental satisfying of urges between a man and a woman was obviously, to Maddy, something else altogether. Like the romantic her sex so often tended to be, she'd taken what had been good—make that great sex—and turned it into something rosy and mystical and everlasting. Something to be tied up with white lace and orange blossoms and rice.

"I'm not ready for marriage, Maddy," he said, feeling he owed her the truth but wanting to put her down gently. The strange thing was that even as he was pushing her away, he felt a desperate urge to pull her back.

"Marriage?" She watched the cool, remote look come back to his eyes, telling her that he was moving even further away. Such remoteness, so soon after their lovemaking, hurt. It hurt like hell. "Who said anything about marriage?"

The sexual languor disintegrated. Pushing himself up to a sitting position, Sax dragged his hands through his hair. "Didn't you?"

"No. I merely said I thought I was falling in love with you. Is that a crime in Oregon, Officer?"

Her scathing tone got beneath his skin. Gritting his teeth, Sax tried to picture his mermaid as she'd been earlier—all warm and sweet and inviting.

"Maddy." He used the same calmly authoritative tone that he'd employed on more than one occasion to convince a perpetrator to put down a loaded gun. "Sweetheart, let's not fight about this."

"Don't you dare *sweetheart* me," she flared, hating his tone. It was the same one her father had always used when he thought he could use police tactics to control his daughter.

Her earlier pain was slowly being replaced by an enervating cold that left her numb. She wouldn't embarrass herself further by crying, Madeline vowed. Because if she did, she might never stop.

"I offered you a gift, Sax. That was all it was. A gift. It doesn't come with strings and it doesn't demand promises." She took a deep breath and closed her eyes. She recognized what she was feeling, realized that it was grief. When she opened them again, her gaze was steady, her expression less tense.

Her eyes drifted from his stony, set, yet strangely vulnerable face to his chest. The furious red line would some day fade to a faint white, making it difficult to see that he'd once been so critically wounded.

But other scars didn't heal so nicely. She knew that it might be a very long time before Sax was able to be close to anyone. Before he could find the strength and the nerve to let anyone into his damaged heart. Before he could love.

Fortunately for him, Madeline considered, she was discovering that she was a very patient woman.

"Actually, to tell you the truth, I didn't even plan to say it," she said, her gaze returning to his face. "But I did, and it felt immensely right at the time, so now you can either accept it or throw it away, but you can't give it back."

"But I don't have anything as valuable to give you in return."

"You saved my life," she reminded him. "I'd say that's a pretty good start. And if you still want to try to top that—" she wrapped her arms around his neck and pulled him down on top of her "—I've got a few suggestions along that line."

Her smile was contagious, lifting the dark cloud that had enveloped his heart. "My God, woman," he said, feeling his body respond to the soft feminine shape beneath him, "don't you ever get enough?"

"Of you?" She pressed a hard kiss against his mouth. "Never."

She wrapped her arms around him, inviting. Accepting. And as he took them both quickly into the mists, Madeline told herself that it was enough. For now.

8

IT WAS THE SUNSHINE that woke her; the warm, buttery rays slanting into the room were the first she'd seen in nearly a week. Sax's strong arms were still around her, his long legs flung carelessly over hers, pinning her to the bed. Looking up, she met a pair of smoky gray eyes that were warmer and less guarded than she'd ever seen them.

"Good morning, mermaid." Sax ran the back of his hand down her cheek.

"Mmm." She snuggled closer. "I don't ever want to move from this spot."

He couldn't think of a better way to spend the rest of his days. Or his nights. "The storm passed." He brushed her tumbled hair away from her face and kissed her temple.

"Mmm." His touch was extraordinarily gentle for such a large man. Especially one whose glower could probably cut through granite. Madeline closed her eyes and sighed as a slow pleasure rippled through her.

"The water should be down enough at low tide to take the launch into town."

She squeezed her eyes even tighter at the unwelcome news. If she hadn't been so unhappy, she would have noticed that Sax's voice was as gritty as sand. Six days ago she couldn't wait to get off this jetty; now she didn't want to ever leave.

"How much time do we have?"

He glanced over at the bedside clock, calculating the hours remaining before they would have to rejoin the real world. Experiencing a raw feeling of possessiveness stronger than anything he'd ever known, he dived his hands into her hair and said, "Time enough."

Giving herself up to the power of his desperate kiss and clinging to him as if she'd never let go, Madeline allowed herself to fly. To dream.

THERE WAS A RESTLESSNESS in Sax; Madeline sensed it all morning long. After the initial explosion last night, his subsequent lovemaking had been tender and leisurely. But this morning she'd sensed a simmering violence just beneath the surface. A violence born of frustration. And, she feared, of regret.

She stood out on the observation deck, watching him walk back from the boathouse where he kept the launch that would serve as her transportation off the island. He was walking with long, purposeful strides, but his dark head was lowered and his hands were thrust deep into his pockets. He reminded her of a caged animal. Even from this distance, Madeline could feel his vexation. And his resolve.

He'd take her to the mainland and hand her over to the proper authorities. But then, she knew, he would turn his back and walk away from her. From what they might have had.

Lifting her gaze from Sax, she looked out over the sea. Overnight the water had turned from an angry, sullen gray to an exuberant blue. The waves were sun brightened and almost glassy this morning. For the first time since she'd awakened to find herself off the Oregon coast, the ocean reminded her of home.

Home. Additional memories came flooding back: pleasure boats skimming across sparkling waters, their colorful sails snapping in the ocean breeze, a city skyline, the dark green of a park, the curving strands of gleaming sand, glittering like diamonds beneath a bright yellow sun.

"You look as if you're a thousand miles away." The deep, wonderfully familiar voice captured her attention, bringing her out of the pleasant reverie.

She spun around, joy shining on her face and in her eyes. Sax was lounging against the doorframe in his quiet, dangerous way. "Not quite that far. I suddenly remembered where I live. Where my home is."

Your home is here with me, Sax wanted to say. But it would be a lie. The past six days, especially last night, had been a pleasant respite from reality. Now that the storm had passed, it was time to face some serious truths.

"Where's that?" He gave himself points for sounding nonchalant when he wanted to tie her to the bedposts and never let her go.

"San Diego." Her smile, brimming with self-satisfaction for finally having remembered, rivaled the rare sunshine. "I'm from San Diego," she repeated. "And I work for the *San Diego Union.* The police beat."

"The police beat?"

He arched a brow. Most of the police reporters he'd ever met were grizzled newspaper veterans who wore rumpled twelve-year-old suits, smoked cheap cigars and liked their whiskey neat. And often. They favored old-fashioned notepads over computers for writing their stories, spent an inordinate amount of time hanging around bars frequented by beat cops and detectives alike, and he had always suspected that most of them harbored a secret yen to be cops themselves.

None of them—at least none of the ones he'd ever met—possessed thick, wavy hair, wide, wonderfully expressive eyes or could make a faded police T-shirt look as good, not to mention as sexy, as this woman standing in front of him did.

"The police beat," Madeline repeated firmly. That stubborn little line that he found both irritating and endearing appeared between her brows. She folded her arms over the front of an ancient black Oregon State sweatshirt. "Got a problem with that, Officer?"

"Not at all," he said, not entirely truthfully. "I just figured you more for the society pages."

She opened her mouth to blast him with a scathing response, then, just in time, she caught sight of the twinkle in his gray eyes. "Unfortunately I have an allergy to charity galas, society lunches and debutante balls." She gave him a sweet, false smile. "It must be my plebian upbringing."

If she was telling the truth, she wasn't giving herself enough credit, Sax considered. Because the unpalatable fact was that despite having grown up in the middle-class environment of a cop's household, he could easily see her dressed in silk and expensive scent, entering a ballroom on the arm of a ridiculously handsome escort.

Even now, dressed in his ancient sweatshirt and jeans, with her russet hair fanned by the sea breeze, she exuded more class than all of the society matrons Ellen kept insisting on introducing him to.

When he told her what he was thinking, Madeline smiled. Then, spanning the small space between them, she lifted her palm to his cheek. "How's the tide?"

"Getting lower by the minute."

"Would you think me terribly forward and wanton if I told you that I want to make love with you again? Before we have to leave?"

"Terribly forward." He lifted her into his arms, surprising her with the romantic gesture. "And decidedly wanton. Remind me one of these days to tell you how much I like forward, wanton women."

Twining her arms around his neck, Madeline laughed merrily as he carried her effortlessly back into the lighthouse.

Unlike their first, wild coupling last night, Sax undressed Maddy with care. Slowly, lingeringly, pausing to give pleasure then take it in return.

With each touch of his hands on her warming flesh, with each caress of her lips against his taut body, they brought each other to new heights of pleasure that neither had known existed. Long, lingering strokes, whispered caresses. Their lips touched, then drew apart to murmur foolish endearments, rash, inarticulate promises, then touched again.

When finally he slid effortlessly into her, claiming her, her name was on Sax's lips. As she wrapped her arms around him, welcoming him into her warmth, his name was on hers. Together they soared, hands linked, lips fused, until at last they lay still, hounded by unhappy thoughts that came crashing back before their hearts had returned to normal rhythm.

Unwilling to completely give up physical contact, Madeline and Sax held hands as they lay side by side on their backs, staring up at the whorls in the white plaster ceiling.

"You never told me," he said, "what story you were working on for the *Union*."

If she'd been hoping for a declaration of undying love, she would have been disappointed. If she'd been waiting for him to ask her to stay here with him, she would have felt defeated. Telling herself that she'd expected nothing, but knowing deep down inside that was a lie, she felt more than a little depressed by the way he'd managed to pick up their earlier conversation so easily after what had been for her a remarkably intimate experience.

"That's because I don't remember."

Sax didn't want to talk about her damn work. He didn't want to discuss what she was going to do once she left the lighthouse. And him. During the past days that he'd suffered, frustrated from wanting her, Sax had managed to convince himself that once he'd bedded his mermaid, once he'd experienced the pleasure he knew she could bring to lovemaking, he'd be satisfied. And once that sexual gratification had been fulfilled, he'd be able to put the woman out of his mind and get on with his life.

But something had gone wrong. Because, for some reason he could not understand and was perhaps afraid to contemplate, the more he made love to Maddy, the more he wanted her. The cycle had escalated until it was in danger of spinning entirely out of control.

In order to regain order and hoping to bring some much-needed discipline to both his turmoiled mind and his aching body, Sax decided that for the next few hours, until he watched her walk out of his life for good, he would return their relationship to a less intimate footing.

He shrugged as he forced himself to release her hand and leave the bed. "Well, that shouldn't prove too much of a problem. When we get to Satan's Cove, you can call the *Union* and ask your editor what you were working on." He picked up his briefs from the floor and pulled them up his legs. "Then, once you know that, we can figure out what to do next."

"We?"

He located his chambray shirt, turned it right-side out and put it on. "Someone tried to kill you. I'm not going to let whoever it was have a second shot."

"I'm not your responsibility."

"Aren't you?"

She lifted her chin. "No. I'm not."

He paused in the act of buttoning the shirt and swore softly. Leaning down, he curved his long, dark fingers around her bare shoulders. "Look, Maddy," he said on a low, deep tone that was more dangerous than the loudest shout, "I realize that I'm not exactly anyone's idea of a knight in shining armor. But, dammit, I'm not going to walk away and leave you to handle this by yourself. So you're stuck with me, lady. Whether you like it or not."

"Better the devil you know?" Madeline murmured. She stared up at him, wishing she could see inside his head, wishing she could find that soft, giving spot he tried so hard to conceal.

"Something like that."

"But I don't know you."

He gave her a long look. "No," he agreed at length. "I suppose you don't."

Madeline reminded herself that Sax had obviously spent a very long time building those walls; that being the case, she couldn't expect to pull them down in just a few days. Even if she wanted to. Which, Madeline admitted, she wasn't all that sure about herself.

True, she and Sax had worked remarkably well together. But this lighthouse wasn't the real world. The sex was, admittedly, good. Better than good, she considered—it was like nothing she'd ever known. But you couldn't base a relationship solely on shared work and sex.

There had to be more. There had to be love. And as much as she would have wished otherwise, she wasn't certain that Sax was capable of such a selfless emotion.

The mattress sighed as he sat on the edge of the bed. He pushed her hair back from her serious face until only his palm framed it. "You want to know about me, mermaid? Are you sure you really want to know what crooked roads brought me here?"

One look at his sober gaze, and Madeline's mouth went dry. She swallowed. "I think I do," she said quietly. She had a feeling that if she could only get inside his head, she might be able to figure out how to get inside his heart.

"Ah, Maddy." Sax shook his head. This woman stirred thoughts he couldn't afford; she encouraged dreams that only a starry-eyed optimist could hope for. "If you make a habit of prying into people's private corners, I can understand why someone was trying to kill you."

Despite his vow not to become emotionally involved with this woman, Sax couldn't ignore those deep-seated traits of duty, responsibility, drilled into him since childhood, which made him care about her safety. That's all it was, he told himself. That was all he could allow it to be.

She thought she saw a flash of caring in his eyes. But then it was replaced by that faraway remoteness she'd come to despair.

"I didn't always want to be a cop," he said. "When I was five, I wanted to be a cowboy. When I was seven, I thought it would be neat to be a fireman. When I was nine, my life goal was to play center field for the Yankees. And be voted MVP in the World Series."

Madeline smiled and covered his hand with hers. "Oh, it's too bad you didn't make that one. I think I'd like making love to a famous baseball star."

"Vixen." His own lips curved as he touched them lightly, briefly, to hers. "Next time you can wait for Don Mattingly to pull you out of the water."

"There won't be a next time. And even if there was," she decided, "I can't think of anyone I'd rather have save my life than you."

Her soft lips plucked invitingly at his. When Sax felt himself wanting her again, he drew away and forced his mind back to the topic at hand. "By the time I was ten, I'd decided to be a doctor. Like my dad."

"Your father's a doctor?"

That's where he had gotten his deep-seated caring streak, Madeline decided. From his physician father. She could picture Sax, at first appearance seeming dark and forbidding in his starched white coat, but behaving toward his patients with genuine warmth and sympathy.

"Was. He died the summer I turned twelve."

"Oh, Sax. I'm sorry."

"So was I." His expression was as grim as she'd ever seen it, his eyes stormier than she'd ever witnessed. "We were living in Eugene, in a big white house high in the hills, with a wide front porch and two elm trees in the backyard. Mom was on the University of Oregon faculty. She was an artist. A sculptor, actually.

"She was a Creole, from Louisiana, but when she married my father and came to Oregon, she fell in love with the Northwest's native art and had begun to garner a reputation as a folk artist herself. In fact, they were coming home from a gallery opening of her wood carvings when it happened."

His gaze drifted out the window, but as she watched his lips tighten and his eyes narrow, Madeline realized that he was not seeing the bright blue-green waters of the now-calm Pacific. Rather, he was seeing his parents as he'd last seen them so many years ago.

"The cop who showed up at the door to break the news said that the other car crossed the line without giving them time to get out of the way. The driver was drunk—miraculously he survived. My parents didn't."

"Oh, Sax." Tears sprang to her eyes. Madeline remembered with vivid detail how devastated she'd been when her mother had died. But she had been eighteen, a very important six years older than Sax's tender twelve. And her mother had been so ill for so long that in many ways her passing had been almost a blessing.

And most importantly, she considered, she'd had her father, who, despite his own grief, had proved to be a rock. How tragic it must have been to lose both parents in one cruel twist of fate.

"How terrible for you."

"I was so damn angry." His voice was flat and emotionless. "Angry at that drunk driver, angry at the people who'd had the party where he'd drunk too much in the first place, angry at God for letting something like that happen and angry at my parents for going away and leaving me all alone. And angry at myself for not being able to do anything to change things."

"Those are all normal feelings." She put her hand on his arm. A muscle tensed beneath her fingertips, but he didn't pull away. "I would have felt the same way."

He smiled at that, a harsh pull of the lips that held not a spark of warmth or humor. "I doubt if you would have reacted quite the way I did."

"You turned into a hellion," she guessed.

He glanced at her in surprise. "That's right. How did you know?"

She shrugged. "You were a young boy facing a tragic, inexplicable loss. It would only be natural for you to strike out in the only way possible."

"They sent me to live with my grandmother," he revealed. "My mother's mother. My only other relative was an aunt who was too busy traveling around the world to settle down and take care of an orphaned kid.

"Grandmère lived in New Orleans, in the French Quarter. She wasn't young—at the time, she seemed ancient—but looking back, I realize she was in her midsixties. Anyway, it had been a long time since she'd had a child living under her roof. And I was definitely a more difficult disciplinary problem than my well-behaved, convent-schooled mother had been.

"Every day I'd ditch school and wander the Quarter listening to the street musicians. Every night I'd sneak out of bed and shimmy down the wrought-iron railing of my balcony to roam Bourbon Street and pick the pockets of drunk tourists."

"You were a pickpocket?"

"And a damn good one, too." Madeline was surprised that he sounded actually proud of that fact. "I managed to go nearly two years before I got caught."

"I suppose that explains it," she decided mildly.

"Explains what?"

"How such a strong man can have such a soft, tender touch." She surprised him by smiling. A soft, satisfied feminine smile that took some of the edge off Sax's remembered pain. "To think that I have juvenile delinquency to thank for your lovemaking talents."

He shook his head. "Talk about making lemonade out of lemons. Are you always so optimistic?"

"I think so." She must be, Madeline considered. To even allow the distant hope that she might be able to forge a future with this closed, self-contained man. "You were about to tell me how you got caught."

Sax shrugged. "I made the mistake of taking the wallet from an undercover cop. The mayor was running for reelection and was worried about the rash of crime. Since the police chief was the mayor's brother-in-law, he immediately established a street-crime squad. I was their first pinch."

"That must have made the mayor and the police chief very proud," Madeline murmured. "Bringing a fourteen-year-old pickpocket to justice. Couldn't they find an eleven-year-old shoplifter?"

"Hey, I was committing a crime, Maddy. Whatever my age, I deserved to be arrested. Besides, what they did to me down at the station wasn't nearly as rough as what my *grandmère* did," Sax said. "She gave me such a caning that I couldn't sit down for a week."

Madeline winced at the idea of such harsh corporal punishment. "Isn't that a bit severe?"

Sax shrugged. "I needed it. I'd been wallowing in self-destructive grief for two years. If I'd kept on that way, I probably would have ended up in federal prison."

"I honestly can't imagine you in prison."

"Neither could I," Sax agreed. "Especially after the arresting cop dragged a bunch of us kids off to visit one." This time his smile held a faint, reminiscent humor.

"It was the single most frightening day of my life. There we were, eight smart-mouthed, smart-ass street kids, thinking we were the toughest things in the Quarter. We were actually swaggering as we walked into that joint.

"But after four straight hours of having real cons screaming in our faces about how we were nothing but scum and how we were going to end up just like them, we were all bawling like babies. I, for one, decided on the spot to clean up my act."

"I can understand that," Madeline said. "But why did you decide to become a policeman?"

"The guy whose pocket I picked took an interest in me," Sax revealed. "He started taking me fishing, to Saints games, or sometimes we'd just hang around, talking about guy stuff. The kind of things I couldn't talk about with my *grandmère*."

"Such as girls? And sex?"

Sax grinned. "Yeah. That sort of stuff. Gabriel taught me a lot, but I worked on honing my technique myself."

"And you succeeded, very well," Madeline allowed.

He lowered his head and brushed a quick kiss against her smiling mouth. "Thank you, mermaid. That's exactly what you're supposed to say.

"So," he said, finishing up his story, "since I spent so much of my teenage years with cops, I just decided I liked the life, the camaraderie, and most of all, the work.

"I developed a typical white-hat, black-hat mentality. I wanted to spend the rest of my life rounding up all the bad guys and putting them behind bars.

"I returned to the Northwest to go to college, then, after graduation, I joined the Portland Police Department."

"Which you eventually quit," she prompted, wondering if this was where she was going to learn the details surrounding that vicious scar bisecting his chest.

"Which I quit," he agreed abruptly. His eyes shuttered again, like a window painted black. "But that's a story for another time." He ran his hand down her hair. "The tide's down—we'd better get going."

She wanted to protest; she wanted to hear the story of what had brought him here to his isolated lighthouse. She wanted to understand what had turned a dedicated, driven man into a virtual hermit. She wanted to know what had happened to give him not only those visible outer scars, but the inner ones, as well.

But she'd learned to recognize that unrelenting tone in his voice, had come to understand the resoluteness in his gaze. Once again realizing that she possessed a very strong impatient streak, Madeline reminded herself that at least Sax had promised that there would be another time to tell that story.

And that, Madeline decided philosophically, was something.

THE TRIP from the lighthouse to the dock took only fifteen minutes. When the launch first started out, Madeline's stomach twisted into a tight cold knot. The last time she'd been on a boat, she'd almost died. All-too-vivid memories of the terror of that ill-fated excursion started her trembling.

"It's okay." Sax put his arm around her, drawing her close. "You survived that trip, Maddy. I promise this one won't prove nearly as eventful."

"I remember his face," she murmured, staring out at the whitecapped water.

"Whose face?"

"The man with the gun." She closed her eyes, squeezing them tight in an attempt to erase the frightening visage. "I can see him as if he's standing right here in front of me."

"But he's not here." His arm tightened reassuringly, and his lips brushed against her temple. "From the pieces of that boat that washed up onto the jetty, it's a good bet that he drowned in the storm."

Just as she would have. Had it not been for Sax.

The man had saved her life. Was she, she wondered, mistaking her feelings of gratitude for love?

No, Madeline decided as the launch plowed through the choppy waters. What she felt for Sax was real. She risked a glance upward, and as she felt herself drowning once again in his fathomless gray eyes, she wondered how she was going to get along without this man.

Not, she reminded herself firmly, that she'd ever had him. Sax was like the storm that had kept them together on the jetty: dangerous and exhilarating. And like that storm, he would move on, out of her life.

As they made the crossing to the mainland, it crossed Madeline's mind that although they'd not been stranded all that far from the coast in physical distance, during those six days they'd spent together, she and Sax could have been on another planet.

But now, as much as she hated the idea, it was time to return to the real world.

9

THE COASTAL HILLS WERE covered with bright yellow blooms.

"Oh, those flowers are so lovely," Madeline breathed, her wide-eyed gaze taking in the rugged rocky coastline, the towering sea stacks and the buttery-yellow-adorned hills. Although the rocks and sea stacks had become a familiar sight, fog and rain had cloaked the rest of the land.

"It's gorse," Sax told her. "The stuff was imported from Ireland a century ago by an Irish immigrant. The guy supposedly planted it to check the wind erosion on his property. Unfortunately the damn stuff is a weed—it's spread all up and down the coast."

"But it's so pretty," Madeline argued. "I can't see anyone complaining. Especially if it stops erosion."

"You wouldn't have thought it pretty if you'd lived in Satan's Cove sixty years ago. Gorse is an evergreen, and one summer, during a drought, the stuff dried out so much that it caught fire and burned down the entire town. Including an old Victorian whorehouse down by the docks. That proved such a blow for the fishing industry, the town never did entirely recover."

"I don't see how..." Her voice dropped off as comprehension dawned. "All the fishermen left."

"Disappeared like footprints in the sand at high tide," he agreed. "Historians tell of a sudden influx in population to Tillamook, Seaside and Astoria about that time," he said, naming three nearby coastal towns.

"By the time the city fathers rebuilt the town in the mid-thirties, prohibitionists had joined forces with a group of religious fanatics to make certain that no bars or houses of ill repute were rebuilt in Satan's Cove.

"By the time World War II ended, alcohol had returned without much of a battle. So did sex, of course, but these days it's free. Or so they tell me."

She gave him a vague smile, remembering what he'd said about the willing women of Satan's Cove who'd invited him into their beds. But in truth, her mind wasn't entirely on his history lesson; something was teasing in some far, dark corner of her memory. Something that she felt she could almost reach out and touch. Unfortunately *almost* was the key word; whatever it was remained frustratingly out of reach.

"Are you all right?" She was staring right through him.

"What?" Madeline blinked. "Oh, I'm sorry, Sax. What were you saying?"

"I asked if you were all right."

She gave him another absent smile that did nothing to reassure. "Fine."

Sax looked inclined to argue. Madeline was grateful when he didn't. Instead, he remained silent and concentrated on bringing the launch up to the dock.

He tied the launch down, then offered a hand to help Madeline out of the boat. The floating wooden dock shifted beneath her feet, and for an instant, she was back on that fishing boat again. The mental image faded, as did her fear. Taking a deep, calming breath, she glanced around at the cluster of buildings surrounding the rocky cove.

"It's very quaint," she murmured.

"It's not exactly the fast lane," Sax said. "But I like it." He headed down the dock, leaving her to follow. "I keep my Jeep in the boathouse. We'll drive to the bar, and you can make your call to the paper."

The boathouse was secured with a large padlock. Madeline watched as he unfastened it then pushed back the large wooden door. There, protected from the coastal salt water, was a gleaming black four-wheel-drive Jeep Cherokee.

She was not surprised when the truck turned out to be locked, as well. She'd already discovered that Sax was not a man who trusted easily. Even here, where he undoubtedly knew everyone in town, where everyone knew him and where a thief would stand out like a swollen red thumb, he continued to lock away his things as if he were still living in the city.

Such innate distrust made her sad.

They drove down a washboard gravel road, turned left at a yield sign riddled with holes from some errant shotgun, then headed down the coastal village's narrow main street. The town was laid out in a crescent, following the curve of the land. Madeline saw a weathered, unpainted cluster of buildings that billed themselves as the Sportsman's Lodge, a white building constructed in the Cape Cod style, whose sign revealed it to be the Gray Whale Mercantile; beside the general store, another sign advertised New Age crystals and palm readings.

Sax pulled the Jeep up in front of Davey Jones's Locker. Years and weather had faded the paint to a silvery gray. "You can make your call here," he informed her. "And we can have lunch. Iris isn't much of a cook, but she can do wonders with fried oysters."

As soon as he made the suggestion, it crossed Sax's mind that the last thing in the world he needed when he was around this woman was oysters. Ever since he'd pulled her out of that tide pool, he'd gone around in a painfully uncomfortable state of semi- to full-alert arousal.

"This doesn't seem like the kind of town that would harbor a car thief," she murmured, watching him lock the Jeep.

"It doesn't seem like the kind of town that would harbor a killer, either," Sax reminded her. "But then again, appearances are often deceiving." That said, he pulled open the door to the tavern and waved Madeline into the building.

Madeline blinked, trying to adjust her eyes to the dim light. Her gaze slowly circled the room, making out the heavy round wooden tables, the paneled walls adorned with mounted fish. A pool table took up the center of the room; in front of a smoky mirror was an L-shaped oak bar.

"Sax!" a deep feminine voice rang out with obvious delight. "Speak of the devil and you'll see the tip of his tail, my daddy always used to say."

The woman behind the bar had a body that would give a *Playboy* centerfold an inferiority complex. She was wearing a black boat-neck sweater studded with fake jewels that glittered like real gems in the smoke-filled room. The welcome in her voice was echoed in her bright emerald eyes and smiling lips.

"Hi, Iris." Sax's greeting, while just as warm, was a great deal less enthusiastic, Madeline noticed. As she watched him rub the back of his neck—a gesture she'd come to recognize as discomfit—and practically shuffle his feet in the yellow sawdust that had been scattered over the floor, she realized he was actually uncomfortable. "It's always nice to see you, too."

A rich, hardy laugh exploded from the barmaid's glossy red lips. "That's my Sax," she said, pushing back a wild froth of copper hair. "Always the master of the understatement."

Her bright green gaze swept over him with a familiarity that caused a slow burn to kindle inside Madeline. As if reading her mind, the woman turned her interested gaze to Sax's female companion.

"Hi," she said with the same warmth she'd bestowed on Sax. "I'm Iris. And where the hell did Sax find you?"

"I'm Maddy." In this environment, her full name would have sounded ridiculously formal, Madeline decided. "And he found me in a tide pool. Sax saved my life after the boat I was on was swamped in the storm."

An auburn brow climbed an ivory forehead. "Are you telling me that you've been stranded out in that lighthouse with this handsome devil for the past week?"

"Six days," Madeline corrected.

"Jeez Louise," Iris complained, her friendly gaze going from Madeline to Sax and back again. "If I'd known it was that easy to get into Sax's inner sanctum I would have drowned myself months ago."

"Iris . . ." Sax said mildly.

Hearing the soft warning in his steady tone, Iris shrugged, causing the sweater to slide off one creamy shoulder. "Sorry." She flashed him a bold, unrepentant grin. "It's just that it's coming as a surprise that somebody finally hooked you, Saxon."

"You've got it all wrong." When a dark red flush rose from his collar, Madeline decided that she rather liked seeing him flustered for a change.

Once again the woman's slow, judicious green gaze moved back and forth between Sax and Maddy. "Whatever you say, Sax," Iris said agreeably. "The papers are going to love this story," she predicted. "Big city or little hick town, it's all the same—folks love reading about a hero."

"The press isn't going to find out anything about this." This time Sax's warning was unmistakably written in stone. "And for the record, I'm no damn hero."

"That's what he keeps saying," Iris told Madeline. "But no one's buying the story. Not after all that went down last year."

She'd definitely piqued Madeline's already stimulated curiosity. "What—"

"Maddy needs to use the phone," Sax interjected quickly. Firmly.

"Sure. Whatever you say, Sax, sweetie."

Another shrug sent the sweater sliding precariously off the other shoulder. As she caught a glimpse of lush, creamy breasts, Madeline couldn't help wondering why on earth Sax had chosen her over this woman's obvious feminine charms. Besides being spectacularly beautiful and having a body that could have easily won her the Miss Universe crown, Iris appeared to be genuinely nice.

"You can use the phone in my office," Iris offered. "It's right down the hallway, past the little girls' room."

"I'd better use the pay phone," Maddy said. "It's long distance."

She didn't have a cent to her name, but figured that the paper would accept the charges. Particularly since whatever story she'd been working on had almost gotten her killed.

"You'll have more privacy in my office," Iris argued. "As for the charges, I'll just add them to Sax's tab." Iris folded her arms on the bar and leaned forward, giving Sax a bird's-eye view of her remarkable cleavage. "You and I can discuss payment terms later, sugar."

As she left the room, Maddy tried to hear Sax's murmured answer and failed. But the sound of his deep laugh, as he responded to something else the female bartender had said, made Madeline feel like crying.

TEN MINUTES LATER Sax found her still sitting behind Iris's desk, her elbows on its cluttered surface, her head in her hands. Comparing her to the woman he'd just left washing beer glasses, Sax was reminded yet again of how small Maddy was.

"Something wrong?"

She took a deep breath and lifted her weary gaze to his. "I talked to Mike McKibbon—he's my editor."

"And?"

"And he doesn't have any idea what I was working on. It seems that I took a leave of absence three weeks ago." Madeline's voice was flat and discouraged. "Mike said that he had the feeling I was on to something hot."

"That's all?"

"No. He also said that when he asked me about it, all I would tell him was that it was personal."

"Damn."

"You can say that again." She closed her eyes.

"Hey, it's only a minor setback." Brushing aside a liquor inventory and a stack of invoices from a Portland wholesaler, he perched on the edge of the desk. "I promise we'll find whoever it was who hurt you, Maddy. You just have to trust me."

"I do."

It was true. He could see her absolute faith shining in her eyes. For some reason he didn't want to think about, such trust moved him more than the desire she'd so eagerly displayed.

"What the hell is it about you?" he murmured, more to himself than to Madeline. "Why is it that whenever I'm with you, I can't stop looking at you? And whenever we're apart, even for a few minutes, all I can think about is you?"

Without giving her time to answer, his mouth settled on hers in a hard, hungry demand. Heat flared instantly. The shared kiss was unabashedly erotic—hot, openmouthed and ravenous.

Wanting—needing—to feel her soft, warm flesh, Sax yanked the sweatshirt up. As his hands massaged her breasts, his tongue dived between her parted lips to taste her sighs. Without taking his mouth from hers, he slid off the desk, at the same time hauling her from the chair. Her avid lips drinking in his dark taste, Madeline went willingly. Eagerly.

She was the most responsive woman Sax had ever encountered. "Ah, Maddy," he breathed, his teeth taking sharp, exhilarating nips of her tender lips, "one of these days you're going to drive me right over the edge."

He spread his legs; his hands trailed down her sides to her waist, his fingers digging into her skin. Then with a masochism he'd never known he possessed, he ground her against his aroused body. Once, twice, then a third time until he was in danger of popping all five metal buttons on his jeans.

"Do you know how close I am to taking you right now?" he growled in her ear. His teeth nipped at the tender skin of her lobe; his tongue swept the pink shell-like interior until he felt her knees begin to buckle. "Right here. On Iris's famous Captain Vancouver desk."

"Sax, we can't." Her weak protest was made on a ragged moan. Her hands combed desperately through his hair, dragging his mouth back to hers.

Sax slid one hand between them, manipulating the fastener on her jeans with a deftness that defied their trembling. The hiss of the metal zipper lowering was unnaturally loud in the stillness of the room. Madeline froze.

She grabbed at the treacherous hand, trying to stop him. "Sax—"

"Don't say anything, love." His hand slid into the denim opening. "Not yet. Let me just touch you. For a minute. Then we'll stop."

When his clever, wicked fingers made their way beneath the elastic leg band of the cotton bikini briefs, unerringly locating the ultrasensitive nub protected by the silky triangle of soft curls, a familiar ache began throbbing inside her. Her fingers dug deeply into his shoulders; she sagged against him, the erotic heat making her knees buckle.

"You're so hot," he murmured wonderingly. "And wet." His fingers caressed the soft, slick petals with a sure, knowing skill, then eased inside her. "Is that for me, mermaid?"

"Yes," she gasped as she writhed desperately against his hand, trying to appease the excruciating ache between her thighs. "Only you."

"Lord, lady, you taste so good." His hands seductively worked their erotic magic while he continued to tantalize her mouth and neck with his mouth and tongue, igniting embers deep inside her. "Like rich warm honey. And sex. And temptation."

When his tongue swept the moist, dark interior of her mouth, she began desperately sucking on it, drawing it deeper between her lips in a way that told him exactly how desperate she was to have him inside her.

"I don't think I'll ever get tired of your sweet, sexy taste, mermaid."

Her own hand thrust between them to move anxiously against his erection. Her uninhibited caress, along with the abandoned mating dance her tongue had engaged his in, nearly pushed Sax over the edge.

His own legs no longer steady, Sax sat down on the brown leather chair, pulling her onto his lap. Maddy's breathing was as harsh and uncontrolled as his. And every bit as ragged with need. Her legs were sprawled over his thighs. Her head was on his shoulder, her hair a tumbled russet cloud. Her eyes, half-closed, were dark, heavy lidded and slumberous. She looked wanton and willing and so exciting that he felt he was going to explode. Sax was aching to plunge inside her, to fill both her body and her soul.

His fingers thrust deeper, stroking, caressing, adoring the very heat of her. She was so wonderfully wet.

So incredibly hot. And all that heat, Sax thought with a flare of pure masculine satisfaction, belonged to him.

"Sax . . . please . . ." Her whispered voice trembled raggedly. Her heated body shivered deliciously.

"Let it happen, love." His deep voice was as warm and soft as ebony velvet and filled with tenderness. "Just hold on to me. I'll keep you safe."

Trusting him implicitly, Madeline's surrender was absolute. Her control deserted her; she gave herself up to the feelings—to the heat, to the power, to her lover.

When she arched against him in sweet release, Sax covered her mouth with his, drinking in her moans.

As she slowly returned to reality, Maddy's first thought was that she should be ashamed of herself for behaving so recklessly. How could she have allowed him—encouraged him, even—to make love to her in the back room of a bar, of all places? Although thankfully he'd managed to display a modicum of restraint, she knew that if he had actually proceeded to take her atop the desk, she would not only have willingly complied, but she would have helped him out of those damn button-fastened jeans that her numbed fingers always had such trouble with.

But it wasn't really her fault, she considered. All he had to do was to look at her or touch her to make all coherent thought disintegrate.

Now that they were back in the real world, she was going to have to work on maintaining some semblance of control, Madeline decided. Making love wherever or whenever the mood struck might be all right in the intimate confines of Sax's lighthouse, but such behavior in public could prove dangerous. Not to mention illegal.

Not wanting to dwell on that negative idea, she allowed her mind to drift, recalling the pleasure of the past minutes in slow, glorious detail.

He'd called her *love*.

Had she imagined it? Had the soft endearment simply been a project of wishful thinking? No. He'd really said it. And since it was the first time he'd uttered that all-important word, Madeline had to infer that it was not simply a convenient response he resorted to during passionate interludes. That being the case, she also refused to accept the possibility that he might have simply slipped and said the first thing that had come to his lust-heated mind. Sax was an expert at keeping a remarkably tight rein on his emotions. So the only logical answer was that he'd really meant it.

"What are you thinking?" He ran a gentle finger down the side of her face. Over the past days, her bruises had faded entirely, revealing the type of peaches-and-honey complexion immortalized by Renaissance painters.

He might have meant it on a subconscious level, Madeline allowed. But from the way his gaze had shuttered again, she decided not to push him into romantic declarations he wasn't yet prepared to make. "Oh, a little bit of this and that."

He traced her upper lip with a fingertip, appearing fascinated by the lush pink bow. "All good thoughts, I hope."

She shrugged.

"Maddy?" Sax prompted softly. His finger rubbed at the faint line that had appeared between her brow. "Is something wrong? Did you remember something else?"

"No." She sighed as she found herself wishing that their physical intimacy could be followed by soft words and promises. Instead, the wall Sax had erected around himself was still there. A bit lower, perhaps. But it was still providing an emotional barrier. "I was just thinking," she murmured, casting a worried glance toward the office door, "that Iris could have come in when we were . . . you know . . ."

"Not a chance." Sax grinned. "I locked the door behind me."

"I didn't see you do that."

He flexed his fingers. "Quick hands."

Not always, Madeline thought. There were times when his hands were deliciously, maddeningly slow. "Well, she's still probably wondering what we've been doing in here all this time."

"Oh, Maddy." He laughed at that, a rich, deep sound she knew would always have the power to thrill her. "I think Iris probably has a very good idea of what exactly we've been doing."

"I was afraid of that." She briefly closed her eyes.

Her cheeks were flushed a bright and pretty pink, making Sax try to recall the last time he'd been with a woman capable of blushing. He came up blank.

"Why don't you call your father?" he suggested with an encouraging smile as he rearranged their clothing. "Perhaps he knows what you were working on."

"I was going to do that," Madeline informed him. "Before you came in and I got all—" she combed her hands through her hair, searching for the proper word "—distracted."

He laughed again. "Anyone ever tell you that you're gorgeous when you're distracted?"

He was more relaxed, more carefree than she'd ever seen him. And if the old glowering Saxon Carstairs was enough to make her heart treble its beat, this new, handsome, smiling rogue was even more appealing. And, in his own way, more dangerous.

Feeling disoriented yet again, Madeline slid off his lap and reached for the telephone. But before she could begin to dial, Sax caught her chin between his fingers and gave her a long kiss that left her breathless.

"Absolutely lovely," he murmured against her tingling lips when the heated kiss finally came to an end. His warm gaze as he looked down into her flushed face turned thoughtful. For one fleeting moment, Madeline thought he was going to say something important. Perhaps even profound.

But in the end, he kept his thoughts to himself. "Call your father." He ran the back of his hand down the side of her face with something that seemed like regret. "I'll order our lunch."

As he left the room, Madeline let out a long breath she'd been unaware of holding. She watched him walk away without looking back, waited until he'd closed the door behind him.

She stared at the telephone for a while, getting up her nerve, trying to figure out how to question her father without tipping him off to her dilemma. As a former cop, he had a built-in radar detector for trouble. A radar that had proved frustrating those few times she and her best friend Patti had stayed out after curfew and found him waiting up for their return.

Finally, with a sigh, Madeline began to push the telephone buttons, dialing the number she knew by heart.

10

AFTER A BRIEF conversation with her father, a few more pieces of the puzzle had fallen into place. When Madeline left the office, she was smiling.

"Must have been good news," Sax said as she approached the table in the corner of the room. Two plates—platters, really—of fried oysters took up most of the small square surface.

"It was." Madeline sat down in the chair he'd pulled out for her. "I didn't want to let Dad know what kind of trouble I'd gotten myself in, so I started out just asking about his honeymoon, the weather, general things like that. Then he asked about Patti, and all these memories came flooding back."

"Patti?"

"Patti's a friend of mine. Four weeks ago I received a frantic, middle-of-the-night call from her." Madeline put the paper napkin on her lap. "The call only lasted a minute, and Patti was whispering, but she said she was in trouble and needed my help."

"She must be a pretty good friend," Sax commented, stabbing a piece of oyster with his fork.

"She's more than a friend. She's like a sister." Madeline smiled, but he could see the little seeds of worry in her eyes. "We were foster kids together. You get close real quickly in a situation like that."

The fork stopped on the way to Sax's mouth. "Wait a minute. I thought your father's a cop."

"He is. But he and my mother didn't adopt me until I was twelve." Madeline picked up the catsup bottle and began dousing her oysters with the rich red sauce.

"The courts took me away from an alcoholic mother when I was five," she continued. "Patti was six when her mother ran off and abandoned her. We were both placed in the same foster home, and although I was technically younger, I always felt like the older sister.

"We spent the next years getting shuffled around from home to home. Our social worker realized that we'd developed a close bond, so she tried whenever possible to place us together."

Madeline's gaze, as she toyed absently with the food on her plate, took on a distant look, giving Sax the impression that she was thinking of a few of the times when the two parentless girls had been forced to separate.

"When we were eleven, we were placed with the Delaneys, and for me, at least, it was as if I'd come home."

"Obviously your folks felt the same way. If they decided to adopt you." Taking on a daughter poised on the brink of her teenage years took more than love, Sax considered. It would also involve a great deal of guts.

"We clicked right away," Madeline agreed.

"What about Patti?"

"Mom and Dad wanted to adopt her, too. But her mother wouldn't sign the papers."

"I thought you said her mother abandoned her."

"She did. But every year or so, she'd be struck with an attack of maternal guilt or remorse or some such thing, and show up again. Just long enough to let Patti think that maybe this time she'd have a real home.

"Unfortunately neither the woman's attention span nor her ability to keep out of trouble was very strong. Inevitably something would happen—a drug bust, or a man, or just the inability to cope—and Patti would be sent back into the revolving door of the juvenile court system."

"That stinks." At least he'd had his grandmother.

"Doesn't it?" Madeline agreed with a soft, sad little sigh. "Anyway, Patti was allowed to stay with us until high school graduation. Then, although Dad offered to pay for her to go to L.A. junior college, she decided the time had come to strike out on her own. She'd always wanted to be an actress. And a singer. So, I went to Northwestern, and she moved to New York."

"Why not Hollywood? Since she was already living in L.A., you'd think that would have been her first choice."

"I think it's because she was brought up in the city that she wanted to get as far away as possible. At any rate, we kept in touch, but over the years, our relationship deteriorated into once-a-month phone calls or the occasional visit.

"Never having had much stability in her life, Patti didn't seem able to stay put anywhere for very long. Or perhaps she inherited wanderlust from her mother. Whatever, she moved around a lot—Boston, Miami, Chicago, Detroit, Seattle.

"The last I'd heard from her—before that middle-of-the-night call—she'd gotten a job singing for a cruise line. That was about three months ago."

"So you told your father about that call?"

"Yes. Well, in a way."

"In a way?"

Madeline looked vaguely guilty. "I didn't want to worry him. You see, I received the call the night before he was supposed to get married. If he even suspected that I was looking into anything dangerous, he'd call the ceremony off and start playing cop again.

"So I told him that I was going out of town for a few days because Patti had gotten herself into a little personal trouble. Which," Madeline defended her actions when Sax gave her a sharp expression, "wasn't all that uncommon. Like her mother, she seems to have an unerring instinct for choosing the wrong man."

Sax wasn't about to touch that comment. Not when he knew how obviously wrong he was for Madeline. She needed a man capable of sticking around for the long haul. He was only capable of living for the moment. She deserved a man who'd love her all the tomorrows of her life.

"I'd guess that you began looking for her at the cruise line," he said, bringing the conversation back to her investigation.

"That's right. And when there was no record of her ever having worked for the line, I got suspicious."

"So naturally you decided to do a little digging."

She plucked a crisp french fry from the woven plastic basket between them. "Of course. I am, after all, a crime reporter."

"I'm still having trouble getting used to that," Sax said dryly. "So do you remember what you found out?"

"Of course." Her eyes were sparkling with avid excitement. "It's a front for a drug-smuggling and prostitution ring."

"Drugs?" Old habits and old interests did indeed die hard, Sax decided. He suddenly felt like a hunting dog at point.

"Drugs," Madeline agreed calmly. "It's all very organized. Young women—most usually women without relatives, or women estranged from their families—are hired as performers to work on the ships going down to Mexico and Central and South America. Some of the women's contracts include an agreement to work in nightclubs down there."

"Clubs that the women belatedly discover, after it's too late to get away, are actually whorehouses," Sax said knowingly. Unfortunately it was a very old and usually successful business. He and Brian had busted a similar ring with ties to the Far East.

"Exactly." Madeline nodded and bit off a piece of french fry. The potatoes were exactly as she liked them, crisp and golden on the outside, tender on the inside. Although the ambience of Davey Jones's Locker left a great deal to be desired, Sax had certainly been right about Iris's being a good cook.

"So," she continued, after she'd finished chewing, "when the performers embark at various ports, the drugs come on."

"I don't suppose you learned how they get the stuff through customs?"

"Of course. Really, Sax," she complained, pointing another fry at him, "I'm very good at my work."

"I'm beginning to see that," he agreed. "So, why don't you fill me in."

"It's quite clever, actually. You see, all the cruises are organized tours. The kind where everything is included—air and ground transportation to the port city, meal vouchers, tips—"

"Baggage handling," Sax guessed.

She rewarded him with a smile. "I knew you were a terrific cop."

"Former cop," he corrected gruffly, irritated by the way her story had started old juices flowing.

"Whatever, you're exactly right. And what makes the entire operation even more safe from detection is that all the cruises are only booked by senior-citizen groups."

"Which would be less likely to be thoroughly checked by customs."

"Exactly."

Something stirred. Something he remembered reading in the *Portland Journal*. But not on the travel pages, Sax recalled. The political page. "I don't suppose you'd happen to recall the name of this cruise line," he said with feigned casualness.

"Of course I do," Madeline agreed. "It's the Paradise Cruise Line. Your golden passport to paradise," she quoted the slick brochure she'd picked up from a San Diego travel agent.

Paradise.. On that fatal day Sax and Brian had learned the hard way that their cover had been blown, one of the unluckier dealers had muttered that single word right before his death. An instant before being wounded himself, Sax, mistaking the man's meaning, had assured the dealer that he was headed in the opposite direction. Damn. How could he have overlooked such an obvious clue? It was a good thing he *had* retired, Sax decided grimly. Because he definitely had lost his touch.

"Sax?" Madeline placed her hand over his clenched fist on the table. "What's wrong?"

"What isn't?" he muttered. "Paradise Cruise Line's executive offices are based in Portland, aren't they?"

"That's right. It's also what I was doing in Oregon. I remember now, Sax." It was excitement, not fear, that had her voice trembling, Sax determined.

He remembered all too well what it felt like to be on a hot trail. He and Brian had felt precisely that way. Right before Brian had gotten killed and he'd come very close to buying the farm himself.

"You'd come to Oregon to confront the owner."

"Martin Hollingwood." She nodded with a grimly fierce determination that allowed him for the first time to imagine her working the police beat.

The man's name was all too familiar. Hollingwood was a self-made man, the type of rugged, pull-himself-up-by-the-bootstraps kind of guy that Oregonians—in particular independent-minded voters—loved to admire. Rumor had the billionaire businessman running for the next available Senate seat.

"I was in Portland to make Hollingwood tell me where Patti was," Maddy divulged.

Nerve. The woman definitely had more than her share of it. Unfortunately she wasn't displaying a great deal of common sense. "I see. And I suppose you expected him just to fall apart at the seams at your accusation, admit to everything and let you just walk out the door scot-free."

"Not exactly," Madeline admitted. "I was hoping that if I got myself hired, I could do a little digging around in his personal files and discover what he'd done with Patti."

"My God." Sax dragged his hands through his hair and stared at her in disbelief. "Why do I have this horrifying feeling that you planned to do exactly that?"

Madeline had two choices. She could be offended by his blatant lack of confidence in her ability, or she could excuse his behavior as concern for her safety and attempt to explain. She chose the latter. "Patti's like a sister to me, Sax."

"I understand that." He leaned toward her over the table, his voice lowered to a rough hiss to keep anyone from overhearing their conversation. "But what makes you think the guy even keeps any incriminating records like that around in the first place?"

"There's always a smoking gun," she said serenely.

His stormy gray gaze mirrored his frustration. "God protect me from idiots and graduates of the Woodward and Bernstein Watergate school of journalism," he appealed.

"Are you calling me an idiot?" That was, Madeline was forced to admit, a quantum leap from *love*.

"If the damn dunce hat fits..." When he saw the hurt flash in her wide eyes, Sax cursed and decided to try again. "Look, sweetheart, I'm sorry. I didn't mean to insult you."

Madeline crossed her arms and gave him a level, accusing glare. "Well, you did."

"It's just that I've had a lot more experience with crime than you have. And believe me, if there was always a smoking gun, we could save the taxpayers of this country a great deal in court costs."

"Well, anyway, since I can't dance or sing, it looked as if I wasn't going to get a chance to infiltrate the company. That's when I came up with the idea of Patti's diary."

"Your friend kept a diary?"

"No. But Hollingwood didn't know that, so I offered to exchange the diary for her."

Sax dragged his hand over his face and swore.

"What would you have had me do?" Madeline argued. "Just ignore Patti's dilemma and leave her to her fate? As horrible as we both know that will be?" Her cheeks were stained with emotion; her eyes flashed golden sparks. "Should I have let Martin Hollingwood keep taking advantage of young, desperate women while he lines his greedy pockets and uses drug money to buy himself a U.S. Senate seat?"

"I would have expected you to take your story to the authorities."

"Sure. And of course they'd believe me, an out-of-town reporter—a female reporter—over a pillar of the community. Not to mention an extremely generous contributor to the Police Benevolence Fund."

Her closed expression told him that she considered those odds slim to none. "You've done your homework," Sax allowed.

"Of course. I've told you, Sax, I am very good at my job. But I'm also a realist and I know that given my word against Hollingwood's sterling reputation, the police would believe image over fact."

It was obvious that she'd braced herself for an argument with him about the impossibility of her claim. Well, Sax considered, she was going to be surprised.

"You never know," he drawled. "Sometimes just when you think you've got them pegged, cops will surprise you."

Her eyes widened. "Are you saying you believe me?"

"Absolutely. I'm also saying that you're right about not letting Hollingwood get away with this any longer."

Hope, mingled with a lingering suspicion that all this was turning out to be too easy, was written across her face in bold script. "Let me get this straight," she said. "Are you saying that not only do you buy my story, but you're actually going to help me bring Hollingwood down?"

"Do I have a choice?" His chair legs scraped across the plank floor as Sax pushed away from the table and stood up. "Come on."

"Where are we going?"

"Portland. We've got some plans to make."

She waited for him to pay Iris, stamping down the tinge of female jealousy when she noticed that he'd added a very hefty tip.

As they left the tavern and returned to the Jeep, Madeline considered that if Sax was looking forward to trapping Hollingwood, he certainly didn't show it. His mouth was set in a grim, unsmiling line, and he proved frustratingly uncommunicative. After several attempts to draw him into conversation, Madeline simply gave up.

But every so often, on the uncomfortably silent drive eastward from the coast, she'd slant a cautious glance at his rigid profile and wished she had even the faintest idea what the man was thinking. He seemed remarkably calm for a man who'd just learned that one of the most respected men in his state was a heinous criminal. There was also no sign of the warm, loving and affectionate man she'd been given such a brief glimpse of.

The grim, uncommunicative Saxon Carstairs had re-turned in spades.

Reckless she might be. But regardless of his unflat-tering accusation, she wasn't a complete fool. It was obvious that he was planning his next move; it was just as obvious that he was not prepared to share his plan with her. At least not yet.

Deciding not to push her luck, Madeline kept her lips pressed tightly together and watched the lush green scenery flash by the Jeep's passenger window.

NEWS OF RECLUSIVE Saxon Carstairs's companion spread through Satan's Cove like a tidal wave. The man hired to find the missing woman felt as if he'd hit the mother lode.

"It's her, all right," he assured his employer from the pay phone outside at the Sportsman's Lodge. "But we've got a problem. The guy's an ex-cop. Name's Carstairs. Saxon Carstairs.

"Yeah, that's right," he answered the rapid-fire query on the other end of the long-distance line. "The same guy that made all the papers. Seems he's living in some lighthouse off the coast. That's where the chick's been this past week, by the way."

Another query. "No, they're not going back there. From what I heard, after they filled the gas tank up on the guy's Cherokee, they headed inland. I figure they're on their way to Portland."

He frowned and rubbed his jaw as he listened to his altered instructions. "Killing a cop, even a retired one, isn't a run-of-the-mill job. I'll need some new papers, a passport and guaranteed safe passage out of the coun-try."

The treacherous deal was concluded swiftly. As the man hung up the receiver, he was smiling.

AFTER THE RUSTIC confines of the lighthouse, Sax's penthouse apartment, on the top floor of the tall glass-and-steel tower overlooking the river, proved a revelation.

"Gracious," Madeline murmured as the private elevator opened directly into the luxurious suite of rooms, "Oregon policemen must receive more generous pensions than the police in California." She stared around at the valuable works of art scattered carelessly over marble tabletops. Museum-framed black-and-white photographs adorned the walls.

"The place belonged to my aunt," Sax said, carelessly tossing his damp jacket over the back of a silvery gray suede chair. "She willed it to me a few years ago." He stuck his hands in the back pockets of his jeans and glanced around. "I guess it is a little impressive at first sight."

"It's a lot more than impressive," Madeline replied. She waded across the plush pewter carpeting to gaze out the floor-to-ceiling windows. "I didn't realize that you were so, well . . ."

"Rich?" Sax filled in for her.

Her eyes directed out onto the river, Madeline only nodded. For the past week, she'd thought Sax to be like her father. A hard-working, middle-class, retired cop. The similarity she'd believed the two men shared had allowed her to feel comfortable—even safe—with Sax, even during those times when her tumultuous emotions had threatened to go careening out of control.

But now, as she took in all these obvious trappings of wealth, she realized that there was a great deal more than just Sax's self-made walls separating them.

"It's happening again, isn't it?" He came up behind her, silent as a cat on the thick carpeting. Wrapping his arms around her waist, he pulled her back against him, nuzzling his chin against the top of her head.

His tender touch was achingly familiar. So why did she feel so painfully uncomfortable? "What?"

A barge loaded with crates was making its way toward the docks. Unwilling to meet what she suspected would be his teasing gaze, she kept her eyes glued firmly to the barge.

"That writer's imagination of yours is running wild." He brushed her hair away from her face and kissed her temple.

A crew of longshoremen had gathered on the dock, waiting to unload the wooden crates. "I don't know what you're talking about."

"I'm talking about the fact that jumping to conclusions often makes for some very unhappy landings." With hands that managed to be gentle yet strong at the same time, he turned her in his arms. "If it makes a difference, mermaid, I'm not rich."

"Sure. All cops live in penthouse apartments on the waterfront. I'm amazed there's not a waiting list a mile long for the job."

Sax was puzzled by her seeming distaste for his home. Most women of his acquaintance had responded precisely the opposite way whenever he'd brought them here. In fact, once he realized that having seen his apartment, they were invariably disappointed to learn his actual net worth, he'd simply stopped bringing women home.

Ellen, naturally, had loved the apartment; she had also loved to entertain, proclaiming it essential in her line of work. For two miserable years he'd been forced to come home from a long shift to find his living room—and all too often his bedroom—filled with guests representing Portland's avant garde art community. The best thing about his divorce, he'd realized after his wife had moved into her own building, was the blessed silence.

"My aunt was rich, Maddy," Sax insisted. "I'm not. Aunt Hannah was a successful photographer. She's the one who got me started taking pictures when she gave me my first camera for my ninth birthday.

"Anyway, when she died, she left me this apartment, her cameras and equipment and some of her photographs, which the will prohibited me from selling, not that I ever would. The rest she willed to various philanthropic organizations."

Madeline studied a cluster of photographs on the adjacent wall with renewed interest. "Your Aunt Hannah was Hannah DuBois?" The renowned photographer was famous, not only for her work, but for her bohemian personal life, as well.

"That's her."

"I attended a retrospective of her work at the Getty Museum a couple years ago," Madeline said. "One of the photographs on display was a portrait of Ansel Adams. Was it true she was with him in Hernandez, New Mexico, when he photographed his famous *Moonrise?*"

Sax shrugged. "That rumor has been around forever, but Aunt Hannah always insisted that a lady never kisses and tells. But she did know Adams. And it's obvious that his style influenced her own work."

"And yours," Madeline murmured. "It's obvious that along with her apartment, you inherited your aunt's talent." Her gaze circled the apartment. "This place is magnificent."

"If you think this is something," Sax said, his lips plucking enticingly at hers, "wait until you see the bedroom."

Her tingling lips curved beneath his tender assault. "You're just trying to seduce me," she accused. The amusement in her voice was also sparkling in her eyes.

"Guilty." He traced her lower lip with the tip of his tongue. A painful, familiar fire had begun to burn in his loins. His hands left her shoulders to caress her back before settling possessively on her hips. He pulled her closer, pressing her intimately against his chest, his thighs, his arousal as he rained hot, wet kisses down the side of her neck. "Is it working?"

The heat radiating from his body made her dizzy. The tenderness in his kisses shimmered through her like golden, liquid sunshine. "I don't know." She moved tantalizingly against him, spreading the warmth. "I think so. But I'm not certain." Madeline pressed her lips against his throat and imagined she could taste the hot blood pulsing beneath her lips. "Perhaps you ought to kiss me again," she suggested silkily. "So I can be sure."

"Whatever you say, mermaid."

He thrust his hands into her hair. But instead of the harsh, quick kiss she was expecting, he appeared content to merely nibble at her lips for a long, seductive time. If he was trying to frustrate her, Madeline decided, it was definitely working. The man seemed determined to kiss her senseless.

His fingers pressed against the back of her head, holding her still while he took his own sweet time ravishing her mouth. When he caught her full, seductive lower lip between his teeth and tugged, she made a soft, sexy whimper deep in her throat. "Sax . . ." She could barely recognize her own voice. It was hoarse and ragged with need. And it was all his fault. Madeline's fingers dug into his shoulders, her lower body moved restlessly, sinuously, insistently against his.

But Sax was determined for once to maintain the upper hand. Every other time he and his mermaid had made love, she'd bewitched him into losing control. But not this time. He was determined to make slow, luxurious love to her no matter how much she provoked him.

He kissed her forehead, her cheeks, the bridge of her nose, her chin. His lips skimmed a trail of fire along her jaw, tasting, teasing before finally returning to her sweet lips. His breath grew ragged; so did hers. And although it was costing him dearly, Sax managed to keep the pace agonizingly slow.

He'd never known that he could suffer so from a mere kiss, had never realized that he could relish such pain born from what should have been only a meeting of the lips. When he finally deepened the kiss, allowing his tongue to accept the invitation offered by her parted lips, he tasted passion, sweeter, hotter, darker than anything he'd ever known. Her soft whimper of feminine acceptance blended with his deep growl of masculine need.

Would he never get enough of this woman? Sax wondered desperately. It appeared not. Because, against all reason, the more he took, the more he wanted.

His lips plucked, his teeth nipped, his tongue plunged, deep and greedy. In turn, her own mouth was hot and avid, and her tongue rubbed brazenly against his. The ache that had been spreading through his groin was now a wildfire. Flames licked at his blood, burned in his loins. His carefully conceived plan to drive her mad with desire had backfired and turned inward on him.

"I was going to show you the bedroom," he rasped on a deep, painful draft of air.

"How far is it?"

"Down the hall."

"I can always see it later." She tugged at his shirt, sending buttons flying across the room. "Because to tell you the truth, Sax, I don't think I can wait that long to have you inside me."

Sax's response was somewhere between a laugh and an oath.

They came together, falling to the floor. Clothes were scattered helter-skelter: her sweater landed on a chair across his room, Sax's jeans ended up on a slate coffee table, followed seconds later by Madeline's. The final barrier between them disappeared as if blown away by gale-force winds, and then Madeline was lying atop him.

"I've never felt this way about anyone before," she said, her voice filled with soft wonder. "I've never wanted any man the way I always seem to be wanting you."

"Join the club, sweetheart." His hands skimmed down her back, cupped her bottom and pressed her hard against him. "Because you've been driving me crazy since that first night."

"Ah, yes." A soft, reminiscent smile curved her lips. "What did you tell me about that night ...? Let's see, something about how good I felt lying on top of you, all warm and soft and naked." When she wiggled her heated body against him, Sax imagined he could see the flare of sparks. "Do I still feel good?"

"What do you think?" he said huskily, biting back a groan.

Her bright eyes laughed down into his. "I think we both feel pretty good," she decided.

"There was something else you told me about that night," Madeline murmured. Her legs were tangled with his. "Something about you wishing that you hadn't had too many scruples just to take me right then and there and end your torment. Do you remember?"

"I seem to recall something about that.... Dammit, Maddy!" Her sinuous movements had him about ready to explode. "If you're going to choose such a damn inopportune time to have a conversation, you're going to have to hold still."

"I'm sorry, Sax." She pressed a hot, wet kiss against his frowning lips. Then his chin. Then, sliding slowly down his body, she teased a trail of stinging kisses down his chest, over the jagged red line bisecting his torso. "But I don't think I can do that."

A low growl escaped from between his lips when her tongue brushed playfully over one of his dark nipples. Somewhere in the dark recesses of his mind, Sax realized that once again, despite the best of intentions, he'd lost control.

Then she blew a soft, warm breath against his stomach, and lower still, parting the crisp dark hair below his belly, and he no longer cared. All he could think about was the molten heat surging through his body.

"You're so hard," she breathed wondrously as she curled her fingers around his aroused length. "And so hot." She began to stroke the rigid flesh. "Did I do this?"

He pressed his heels against the carpet and thrust upward. "What the hell do you think?"

There was a moment's silence as she appeared to be considering what had been, at least for Sax, a rhetorical question. But her hand didn't cease its treacherous caress.

"I think," she said finally, "that you're beautiful. And I love touching you the way that you touch me." Her teeth nipped at the inside of his thigh, drawing a harsh moan. Sax's hands curled into fists at his sides, clutching handfuls of plush carpet.

"And I love the way you taste." Her words hummed against his tightened belly. "I'm so glad that you're mine," she said with a burst of possessiveness that he could recognize all too well.

A drop of moisture glistened on the tip of his sex; when she gathered it in with her tongue, coherent thought shattered. And when she took him fully, deeply in her mouth, Sax closed his eyes and allowed the fires to consume him.

It was agony. Ecstasy. Torture. Bliss. When he didn't think he could last another moment, he shoved his hands through her hair and pulled her astride him.

"I want you so much I ache," he groaned. "But I want to be gentle with you."

"Be gentle later." She clung to him, demanding more. Covering his mouth with hers, entwining her tongue with his, letting him share his taste, Madeline took him fully inside of her. "Because I think I'll honestly die if you don't take me. Now."

Sax's fingers grasped her hips with a force he knew would leave bruises. "So will I, love," he admitted roughly. "So will I."

Her softness was a hot, tight sheath for his power; her knees pressed against his thighs. Sax surged upward again and again, making the fires burn hotter and higher. And still she met him thrust for thrust. Until a burst of blazing ecstasy consumed them both.

Their bodies were slick with perspiration. Madeline was collapsed on top of Sax's chest, and his arms were wrapped around her. He was still inside of her and loathe to leave. A scent that was an evocative blend of him, her and the sweet, musky redolence of their love-making surrounded them.

There were no words for what Sax was feeling, no way to describe an emotion that was so much more satisfying, more all encompassing than mere contentment.

"I think I'm regressing," he managed when he could speak again. His breath was still far from steady.

She snuggled against him. Her eyes were closed, her lashes a lush fringe against her cheeks. "Mmm?"

"Even in my horny teenage days, I never made love to a girl on the rug." The back seat of his *grandmère's* Buick, perhaps, on occasion, but never had he been impatient enough to drag a female to the floor.

"That's because you didn't know me in your horny teenage days."

When she lifted her head and gave him a slow, sexy smile, Sax decided she was right. If he'd met her during those years, he probably would have been crazy enough to risk taking her in crowded Jackson Square during the height of Mardi Gras.

"Besides, I liked it," Madeline admitted.

He ran his hand down her back. "That's because you're not the one with rug burns on your butt."

"Poor baby." Reaching up, she brushed a lock of dark hair off his forehead. "Perhaps a kiss would take your mind off your pain."

Her lips were like a renewed flare of heat as her tongue slid like hot silk between his lips. Sax felt his body stirring to life again deep within her feminine warmth. "I want you again." The incredulity of that shook in his husky tone.

She smiled against his mouth. "Me, too."

"But this time we're doing it right. In a bed. Because I don't think I have any more skin to leave on this carpeting." He rolled over, bringing her with him. When he withdrew, Madeline breathed a soft sigh of regret. "Don't complain, sweetheart." Lifting her effortlessly into his arms, he strode purposefully down a long hallway lined with more of Hannah DuBois's black-and-white photographs. "I promise, you'll love it."

The bed, draped in a black spread, was large and took up most of the room. Madeline laughed delightedly as he dropped her unceremoniously onto the mattress. "Saxon! I can't believe you, of all people, have a waterbed." Waves undulated beneath her.

How could she still think him so stuffy? After all they'd shared. "The doctors prescribed it when I first got out of the hospital," Sax informed her. "They said it would be more comfortable."

Madeline managed with effort to rise to her knees. "Remind me to thank your doctors." She held out her arms.

Sax joined her on the mattress.

And as the shadows grew longer outside the penthouse windows, they lost themselves in heady scientific exploration, discovering the boiling point of water.

11

MADELINE HAD NO IDEA how long she'd dozed when she became aware of Sax's voice coming from the other room.

Leaving the bed, she was aware of a vague ache between her thighs. A slow, reminiscent smile curved her lips. She always felt this way after making love with Sax. She'd never met a more passionate man. And although he wasn't prepared to admit it, a more loving man.

He was on the phone. She stood in the doorway, unabashedly naked, listening to his end of the conversation.

"Look, Ellen, I need to ask a favor."

Madeline was frowning at the idea of Sax's leaving their bed to call his ex-wife when his next words captured her absolute attention.

"Remember that cruise-line guy who wanted to buy my photographs for his ships?

Yeah. Hollingwood. I want you to set up a meeting with him. For this afternoon, if possible."

From the way Sax was thrusting his fingers through his hair, Madeline suspected his request had met with some resistance.

"I know I said that I refused to commercialize my work that way but I've changed my mind."

His firmly cut lips drew into a thin line Madeline recognized all too well. "I'm not hardheaded." His hand made another impatient rake through his hair. "All right, perhaps I can be a bit intransigent from time to time—"

Frustration radiating from every male pore, Sax began to pace. "Dammit, Ellen, we're not married any longer, so let's not get into that again, okay? All I'm asking is for you to arrange a meeting with the guy. At his office. ASAP."

He nodded with grim satisfaction. "Terrific. I'll be here at the apartment, waiting for your call." His stance and his voice softened. "Thanks, babe. I owe you one."

He hung up the phone and became aware of Madeline standing in the doorway. "How much did you hear?"

She folded her arms across her breasts. "Enough that if I were any less self-confident, I might worry about my lover maintaining such a close relationship with his former spouse."

"I told you—"

"I know." Deciding to let him off the hook, she padded across the carpeting in her bare feet and twined her arms around his neck. "Your relationship with your wife is only business." Her breath fanned his neck; her teeth nipped at his earlobe. "Besides, I'm not really worried. Because I have a secret weapon."

She was doing it to him again. His blood was warming, his heart had accelerated, and his entire body was coming achingly, vividly alive. He drew her against him, thinking how perfectly she fit in his arms. As perfectly, Sax considered, as he fit inside the warm silk of her body. "What secret weapon?"

"I intend to leave you so worn out, you can't even think of making love to another woman. Much less pull it off."

"If that's your intention, sweetheart, it's definitely working."

Her flesh, warming beneath his touch, felt like warm satin. Amazingly he was actually considering taking her back to bed again when the shrill bell of the ivory desk phone shattered the increasingly sensual mood.

Swearing, Sax reached over and scooped it up. "Yeah," he barked into the mouthpiece. There was a moment's silence, then a feminine complaint from the other end of the line. "Sorry, Ellen," he said. "I didn't expect you to call back so fast."

He slanted Madeline an apologetic glance. She grinned and ran a fingernail down his bare chest in response.

"I figured he might want to meet right away," he acknowledged. "Yeah, go ahead and make the appointment for six-thirty." He glanced over at the granite clock on the desk. "That'll give me time to take care of a few things first. And Ellen? I really appreciate this." He laughed. "Hell, no, not enough to up your commission. But I'll send you a Christmas card this year, okay? Of course I'll let you know how things work out."

He hung up and immediately began dialing. "Get me MacArthur," he said, dispensing with opening pleasantries. Impatient, he moved from foot to foot as the call was transferred. "Hi, Mac," he said. "I need a favor...."

Madeline couldn't believe what she was hearing. She stomped her foot and shook her head, trying to garner Sax's attention, but he steadfastly ignored her. Finally, matters settled to his satisfaction, he hung up the receiver.

"I don't need a baby-sitter," she flared, turning on him immediately.

"Not a baby-sitter, a bodyguard."

"It's the same damn thing. Honestly, Sax, I'm more than capable of taking care of myself."

He arched a dark, argumentative brow. "The same way you were taking care of yourself the day you ended up on the *Viking Pride?* The day you almost drowned?"

"So I miscalculated a bit."

"How about a lot?"

"All right. I never expected that Hollingwood would actually kill to protect his secret."

"For a police-beat reporter you sure are naive," he muttered what he'd been thinking since discovering what his mermaid actually did for a living.

"I prefer to think that I don't go through life always looking for the worst in people. Like some people I know."

"At least I'm not disappointed," he countered.

"It's still a terrible way to live. Honestly, Sax," she complained on a frustrated huff of breath, "you're the only man I've ever met who smells flowers and immediately starts looking around for the funeral."

"Wrong." Sax didn't want to fight. Not now. Not when he had to leave in a few minutes. "When I smell flowers, I immediately start looking around for a sexy mermaid with hair the color of autumn leaves and eyes that remind me of gold-flecked brandy."

"Well." The irritation drained out of her. "That's probably the most romantic thing you've said to me since you pulled me out of that tide pool."

"Then I've been remiss." He drew her back into his arms and stroked the last of her tension away. "Because you are truly the loveliest, softest, not to mention the sexiest woman I've ever met. And if we weren't going to have company any minute, I'd drag you back to bed and show you that there are some things I can be optimistic about."

She sighed and pressed her lips against his neck. "I still don't understand why I need a bodyguard."

His fingers curved around her upper arms, and he put her a little away from him. "Because the only reason a busy guy like Hollingwood would have agreed to meet with me so quickly is that he's found out you're with me."

"But how—" Comprehension dawned. "Are you saying he had his henchmen in Satan's Cove looking for me?"

"Hollingwood didn't get where he is today by leaving any loose ends dangling, Maddy. Obviously he wanted to ensure that when you did wash up after that storm, you weren't in any condition to do him any damage."

"So what are you going to do?"

"The same thing you were. I'm going to offer to exchange the diary for your friend. Then I'm going to make certain that the bastard is put away behind bars for the rest of his life."

His tone was dark and dangerous and edged with a gritty passion that frightened her. "This is somehow personal, isn't it? Beyond what you feel for me."

He nodded. His eyes, Madeline noted, had lost every iota of softness and warmth and were as hard and flinty as they'd been when she first met him. "I told you that although the guy who killed Brian and shot me was convicted, we never caught the kingpin."

"That's right." Her brown eyes widened. "Are you saying that Hollingwood—"

"That's exactly what I'm saying. And now I'm going to make certain that the bastard pays for hurting two people I've cared deeply about."

It was the closest he'd come to admitting exactly how much he felt for her. Maddy assured herself that once this was over, Sax would be able to say the words she knew he was feeling. Words she'd been waiting to hear.

"I want to come with you."

"No." Releasing her, he gathered up her scattered clothing and shoved it into her arms. "You'd better get dressed. The guy Mac's sending over should be here any time."

As if on cue, the buzzer rang and the doorman announced Sax's visitor. "I'll be right down, Ernie," Sax answered the disembodied voice. To Madeline, he said, "Get dressed. I'll be back in a couple of minutes."

Frustrated but knowing that this was no time to argue, Madeline began throwing her clothes back on with an angry haste that nearly equaled the speed in which they'd been discarded.

THE PLAINCLOTHES COP Sax returned with was young and obviously eager to earn his hero's approval. He listened, nodding enthusiastically as Sax explained that absolutely no one should be allowed into the apartment. And that under no conditions should he let Madeline out of his sight.

"Don't worry, sir," he assured Sax. "The lady's safe with me."

Sax gave him a long, level warning look. "That's what I'm counting on, Murphy." When his gaze moved to Madeline, standing across the room by the bank of windows, his expression softened slightly. "I'll be back before my meeting."

"Fine." She refused to smile. If he didn't care enough to fill her in on what had originally been her own investigation, she was damned if she was going to grovel and beg him to tell her where he was going or what he was up to.

The fleeting tenderness in his face was replaced by that all-too-familiar grim look. "Don't let me down, Murphy," he said. And then he was gone.

Although the young man tried his best to engage Madeline in conversation, she was in too bad a mood to respond. She spent the first ten minutes of Sax's absence pacing the floor. When she passed an ebony-framed bevel mirror hung over an ebony breakfront, Madeline stopped dead in her tracks. No wonder Sax didn't want to take her anywhere in public, she considered. She looked like some backwoods urchin.

Her hair was frizzy from the humidity, and she didn't have on a speck of makeup. She was wearing Sax's Oregon State sweatshirt over her jeans; the black-and-orange shirt was oversize, hanging to her knees, rendering the feminine body underneath shapeless.

She returned to the window. Just as she thought she'd remembered, there was a three-story brick department store across the street. "Come on, Murphy," she said, "we've got some important errands to run."

"But Miss Delaney—" Murphy leaped immediately to his feet "—I'm not supposed to let you leave this building. I gave Officer Carstairs my word," he reminded her.

"You gave him your word that you wouldn't let anyone in," Madeline argued. "And that you'd keep your eye on me. Which you can do while we go shopping."

"Shopping?" He stared at her as if she'd just grown an additional two heads. "You want to go shopping?"

"That's right." She rewarded him with a dazzling smile.

"But you can't."

"Of course I can." Her smile lit up her eyes. "Don't worry, Officer," she assured him. "I'm perfectly capable. Why, my father's a cop and he taught me to take care of myself. And besides, you can stand right outside the dressing room."

He would, Madeline decided, prove handy. Since she had every intention of maxing out her credit card, it would be nice to have some strong man around to carry the shopping bags.

She placed her hand on his arm. "We don't have much time if we want to get back before Sax."

He frowned, clearly torn.

"Please?" Maddy asked, hating herself as she fluttered her lashes in the same way that Scarlett O'Hara had used to captivate the Tarleton twins. She'd never approved of women who relied on feminine wiles rather than intelligence. But as she watched the young man slowly succumb, she realized that sometimes feminine wiles were more than a little useful.

"Well, so long as we're back before Officer Carstairs, I guess it would be okay."

She rewarded him with a dazzling smile. "I promise, we'll be back here safe and sound before you know it. And before Sax even knows we've gone."

"I certainly hope so," she heard him mutter behind her.

Although her credit cards had disappeared along with her purse during that failed attempt on her life, such loss proved no problem. Smiling obligingly, the chic woman in the credit office ran her crimson-tinted fingernails deftly over the store's computer keyboard. Bingo. Madeline Delaney's account number instantly appeared on the screen.

Then, with her credit verified, relying on yet another Southern metaphor, Madeline tore through the trendy Northwest-based department store like Sherman marching through Georgia. Ever obedient but constantly fretting, Officer Murphy traipsed along behind her, loaded down with an increasing number of packages. He balked when she'd talked the receptionist at the salon into a shampoo and blow dry, but he lost the argument and ended up hovering over her like an overly protective German shepherd, looking decidedly uncomfortable in the pink-walled, plant-filled room.

They entered the apartment building nearly two hours later, with fifteen minutes to spare.

Unfortunately Sax had returned even earlier.

"Where the hell have you been?" he demanded the moment she entered the lobby. His face was dark, his eyes wild.

"Shopping."

"Shopping?" He stared at her, incredulous. His fingers dug into the shoulders of her glossy new red raincoat. "You risked your life to go shopping?"

"I was tired of looking like Little Orphan Annie," she explained. "And besides—"

"Dammit, Murphy," Sax roared, cutting off Madeline's planned explanation, "you were supposed to be looking out for her."

The young officer's face was so pale Madeline could see a sprinkling of freckles she hadn't noticed before. "Really, Sax," she complained, "Murphy was taking very good care of me. He didn't let me out of his sight once."

Sax ignored her protest. His glare, as it raked over the young man's face, could have sliced granite. "I specifically instructed that she was not to leave this building."

"Actually, Sax," Madeline contradicted, "that's not exactly what you said. Your exact words were—"

"Murphy can speak for himself, dammit!" He crossed his arms, glaring down at the both of them. "He doesn't need you to protect him."

"Of course he doesn't. But neither does he need you yelling at him in public." She slanted a glance toward the doorman. "Why don't we go upstairs and discuss this in private?"

Still glaring, Sax punched the button for the penthouse elevator. When the dark brown door slid open, he gestured them to precede him.

Although he didn't speak on the short ride up to the apartment, the temperature in the elevator had chilled considerably from the last time she'd shared the compact space with him. Madeline decided that if the building had ten more floors she and Murphy would probably have frostbite before they reached their destination.

As soon as they entered the apartment, Madeline turned toward Sax. "Could I please speak with you in private before you finish biting our heads off?"

"Fine." The single word was short and blunt and somehow managed to sound like an oath.

"I'll just put these packages on the sofa," Murphy offered.

Already on their way down the hallway, neither Sax nor Madeline answered.

"Do you realize that I was going crazy?" Sax asked, turning on her the minute they were alone. "Do you have any idea the thoughts that have been going through my mind?"

"I'm truly sorry, Sax." Madeline slipped out of the coat. "But—"

He cut off her words with a vicious swipe of his hand. "You're sorry? That's all you have to say? Dammit, Madeline—"

"I just wanted to look nice for you, Sax," Madeline said softly.

His jaw dropped as she stood in front of him, dressed in a fluffy scarlet angora sweater and a short red leather skirt that hugged her hips and bottom like a lover's caress. The skirt ended at midthigh, displaying firm, slender legs clad in a pair of red ribbed tights. The heels of the crimson suede boots elevated her height by three inches.

"Dammit, you really don't fight fair, do you, mermaid?"

She could hear the lingering frustration in his voice. But a sexual huskiness had crept into his tone, as well, letting her know that his anger had been extinguished.

"Are you saying you like it?" Smiling, she held her arms out and turned around slowly.

"What red-blooded male wouldn't?" Sax stared at her in blatant disbelief. He'd known she was pretty. Hell, there were times, in the right light, when her eyes were glowing with passion, that she'd appeared even beautiful. But he'd never expected that she could look so outrageously, dangerously sexy.

She looked older, too. And more confident. He narrowed his gaze, trying to decide why that was and decided it was because of her hair. No longer flowing free in those wild, uncontrollable waves he loved to wrap around his hand, it had been combed back into the same sophisticated style Ellen had always favored. A French twist, he recalled his former wife calling it. And although it had always suited Ellen's glacial blond image, he hated the style on Maddy.

"The hair's all wrong."

She lifted a protective hand to the sleek twist. "It's the style."

"Not for you."

With an arrogance she knew she should protest, he began plucking pins out, tossing them onto the carpet.

"Those are going to play havoc with the vacuum," she warned him.

"I'll leave a note warning the maid."

The last of the pins fell to the floor underfoot; his wide hands were in her hair, loosening it, settling it down around her shoulders. "That's better."

Her calm eyes met his approving gaze. "You realize, of course, that you had no right to do that."

"I had every right." He lowered his head and gave her a deep kiss meant to vent the last lingering vestiges of frustration and fear. But when desire flared all over again, Sax backed away. "I have to go."

"Please, Sax. Take me with you. It's my story."

His hand tangled in her hair. "I'm not going to let that bastard near you, Maddy. You'll stay here with Murphy until I get back. Then I promise that you'll get an exclusive."

That, Madeline considered, was something, she supposed. "What about Patti?"

Sax knew about best friends. Hollingwood had taken his, but he damn well wasn't going to get Maddy's. "Don't worry. We'll get her back safely. You have to trust me, Maddy."

"I do." It was the truth. Even as she spoke the words, Madeline wished that Sax could trust her enough to open up that secret, vulnerable place in his heart that would allow him to love her.

He kissed her once more, and then he was gone. Leaving her alone again with a severely chastised Murphy.

THE WAITING WAS proving agonizing. Madeline paced the floor, her eyes glued to the clock, waiting for the telephone to ring. What if Sax's plan, whatever it was, had gone awry?

What if Hollingwood had gotten the upper hand?

What if—oh, dear God no!—Sax was dead?

"Nothing's going to happen to him," Murphy assured her after she'd practically worn a path in Aunt Hannah's plush carpeting.

The man clearly admired Sax. It was from him that she'd learned the details of the shooting that had so brutally wounded Sax and killed his partner.

They'd both been undercover for months, Murphy related. Having infiltrated a local syndicate, they'd set up a trap designed to snare the elusive kingpin who'd been flooding the entire Northwest with illegal drugs. But somehow their cover had been blown, and it turned out to be the cops who'd walked into the deadly trap.

"If he's all right, why doesn't he call?" Maddy complained. At that moment, the intercom buzzed, causing the pair to jump.

"Hello?"

"Ms. Delaney?" an unfamiliar voice inquired. "This is Officer Kenyon of the Portland Police Department. May I speak to Officer Murphy, please?"

"Are you calling about Sax?" she asked.

"If I could just speak to Murphy, ma'am," the polite, frustratingly officious voice answered, "I'll be happy to fill you both in at the same time."

"Yeah, Joe," Murphy answered. "What's up?"

"Look—" the deep voice lowered "—I've got an audience here. Why don't you tell the doorman to let me come up and we can discuss this in person?"

Murphy took only an instant to make a decision. "Send the officer up, please," he instructed. He turned to Madeline. "It's okay," he assured her. "Joe's one of the good guys. In fact, he was working on the drug-enforcement squad with Brian and Sax.

"Which is probably why Sax brought him into tonight's scheme. The three of them were like brothers. I imagine Sax realized that Joe would want to get a shot at the guy who was responsible for Brian's death."

"That makes sense," Madeline agreed. But she couldn't stop worrying. If Sax was all right, why would he have sent this Officer Kenyon? Why wouldn't he have come himself?

The answer was too horrifying to contemplate.

"Tell me," she said, the moment the elevator opened and the uniformed man stepped into the room. "Is Sax safe?"

The officer's blue eyes were kind and gentle, reminding Madeline of her father. "He's going to be fine."

"Going to be?"

"He received a bullet wound in the shoulder—"

"Oh, my God," Madeline interjected. "I knew it." Her knees buckled. Murphy reached out just in time to keep her from sagging to the floor.

"It's only a flesh wound," Kenyon quickly assured her. "The doctors just want to keep him overnight for observation, to make certain that he doesn't go into shock."

"I want to go to Sax. I need to be with him."

A smile that belonged in a toothpaste commercial told her that he was one step ahead of her. "That's what I'm here for. I have a squad car downstairs. My instructions were to take Murphy here back to the station and drop him off, then take you to the hospital."

"Can't we go to the hospital first?"

"The station's on the way to the hospital, Maddy," Murphy assured her. "Otherwise, I'd just call a cab."

"Oh." Maddy nodded. "Let me just get my coat and I'll be right with you."

Soon she was sitting in the blue-and-white patrol car as it wove its way through the dark streets.

In the front seat, the two men talked quietly.

Alone in the back seat, Maddy twisted her hands together, closed her eyes and prayed.

She was only vaguely aware of Murphy's departure; his reassuring words, meant to comfort, were an inarticulate buzzing in her ears. All she could think about was getting to the hospital.

To Sax.

Later she would understand that it was her overwhelming concern for Sax that kept her from noticing that they'd reversed direction and were heading back the way they'd come. Toward the riverfront.

Finally, as the car wound its way through the narrow streets, reality sunk in. She reached out, remembering to her dismay that the back doors of police cruisers did not have interior handles. "You're not really taking me to Sax, are you?"

Kenyon shot her a glance in the rearview mirror as he pulled up in front of a large brick building she took to be a warehouse. "On the contrary." He cut the engine, then turned toward her, smiling at her through the black mesh screen between them. The blue steel of the gun glinted with deadly malice in the spreading glow of a nearby streetlight. "I have taken you to Saxon, Miss Delaney. He and Mr. Hollingwood are inside as we speak."

He left the car, then opened the back door. "Let's go," he said, jerking her from the vinyl seat. Both his behavior and his tone lacked their former friendliness.

"We wouldn't want to keep lover boy waiting now, would we?"

Her only thought, as she walked toward the darkened warehouse, was that when she and Sax extricated themselves from this sticky situation, he would probably cheerfully kill her himself for not following orders.

12

KENYON LED MADDY through the abandoned warehouse into an office.

"Well, Ms. Delaney," the man seated behind the desk greeted her, "we meet again." Behind him stood an unsmiling man the size of a soft-drink machine.

Madeline refused to respond, instead directing all her attention to the man sprawled in a chair in front of the desk.

If Sax was at all surprised to see Maddy, he didn't reveal it. His expression remained remote; his eyes did not display so much as a flicker of recognition.

"What's the matter, Carstairs?" Hollingwood's tone was laced with amusement. "Don't tell me that you've tired of your little lovebird so soon?"

"She's not my little lovebird," Sax said. He was looking directly into Madeline's face, but there was no warmth in his gaze. "The woman's been nothing but a problem from the moment she washed up on my rocks. A responsibility I neither wanted nor needed."

His words struck like a lash at her heart. Madeline told herself that he was lying. That he didn't want Hollingwood to know how much he truly cared for her. But then she remembered what he'd once said about unwelcome responsibility.

And she couldn't help but wonder.

"Ms. Delaney can indeed be a vexing problem," Hollingwood agreed. "Still, if you've no personal interest in her, why did you get involved in her foolish scheme?"

"I wanted the diary."

"Why?"

"Because I figured the one thing she had right is that her friend's diary would make your political career disintegrate like a sand castle at high tide," Sax said.

"I hadn't realized you were interested in politics." Hollingwood was passing his leather gloves back and forth from one hand to the other, eyeing Sax intently.

"I'm not. But you are."

There was a moment's silence as Hollingwood mulled over the implications of that remark. "I had Ms. Delaney brought here in order to convince you to trade the diary for her freedom," he mused aloud. "Are you telling me that I miscalculated?"

"Let's just cut to the chase, Hollingwood," Sax barked, allowing a flare of impatience. "The diary's for sale—you want it or not?"

"I don't understand." A frown marred Hollingwood's brow. "My sources at your former precinct assured me that you were not corruptible."

"It's true," Kenyon insisted, speaking up for the first time since he'd brought Madeline into the room. "Everyone in the department, from the commissioner down to the cop on the beat knew that the mighty Saxon Carstairs was a Boy Scout." The scorn in his voice revealed exactly how little he approved of such upright and rigidly moral behavior.

"Yes." Hollingwood smoothed the lapel on his coat, scowling momentarily at a speck of dirt. "That's what I've been led to understand."

"That was before Brian was shot," Sax countered in a calm, reasonable tone worlds away from how Madeline was accustomed to hearing him talk about his friend. "All those months in the hospital, I had time to think. And I realized that all my so-called good deeds hadn't kept me off the critical list, they didn't pay my bills and they damn well didn't fill in the income gap when I was forced to take early retirement.

"Maybe I'm a late learner, but I've come to the conclusion that you and my old pal Officer Kenyon here have the right idea. Money is power, Hollingwood. And you've got more dough than any one man needs. Plus, I figure you owe me for all that lead the doctors dug out of my chest. . . .

"So here's the deal. You get the diary in exchange for a very large case of some of those crisp green bills you're so good at spreading around."

Hollingwood rubbed his jaw and appeared to be considering the offer seriously. "You still haven't suggested what we do with the woman."

"Let her go," Sax suggested with an uncaring shrug. "Without the diary, she doesn't have any proof. It'd just be her word against yours. And we all know who'd be believed."

"Let her go with you?" Hollingwood suggested silkily.

"I told you." Sax's jaw tightened. His dark, emotionless eyes met hers and held. "I don't want her."

"Good," Madeline flared, "because I'd rather die than spend another minute with you. You're a disgusting, immoral man." Pulling away from Kenyon's grip, she marched up to Sax and slapped him against his rigid cheek. "And to think that I trusted you."

His cheek was stinging. Her palm had left an imprint on his dark skin. "That was your second mistake," he told her coolly.

Hollingwood threw back his blond head and laughed, obviously enjoying the performance. "Is there anything more passionate," he said, eyeing Madeline with renewed interest, "than a woman scorned?"

The sudden sound of sirens wailing down the street filled Madeline with hope. Hollingwood stiffened and gestured with his head toward the door. Kenyon left the office, returning a moment later. "It's only fire trucks," he announced.

Madeline's spirits sagged.

The threat of discovery had changed the mood in the room. The humor was gone from Hollingwood's eyes. "Take off that coat," he instructed Madeline. "I'm beginning to think that my plan to kill you may have been a bit hasty." There was a new emotion in his gaze that frightened Madeline even more than the prospect of murder. When she refused to do as ordered, Hollingwood said, "Kenyon, help the lady out of her wrap."

Her eyes were wide and pleaded with Sax as the rogue cop yanked the coat off her shoulders, down her arms and tossed it onto a nearby chair.

"Nice." Hollingwood nodded his approval as his gaze took a slow, treacherous tour over her body, still clad in the clinging soft sweater and short leather skirt. "I think, my dear, that you'll be a very popular attraction in Latin America."

He slid off the desk and ran his hands over her shoulders, down her sides, to her hips. Madeline bit her lip; it was all she could do not to let him feel her inner tremors. His hand cupped her breast and squeezed painfully. "You're a bit thin, but some men prefer a less voluptuous woman."

Releasing her, he then grabbed a handful of her lush dark hair and twisted it around his hand. "Of course, we'll want to dye your hair. Blondes are much more popular south of the border," he told Sax.

"You can dye the stuff purple if you want," he answered, ignoring the hurt and shame shimmering in Madeline's wide eyes. "I just want enough dough to retire in comfort."

"And you'll have it," Hollingwood agreed. "As soon as I have the diary."

"Fine." Sax nodded brusquely. "Let's go."

"Excuse me," Madeline said. "But it's freezing in here. If you're through pawing me, may I put my coat back on?"

"Of course. We wouldn't want you to catch cold."

"You're so considerate," Madeline snapped. Scooping up the abandoned coat from the chair, she threw it over the unsuspecting Kenyon's head.

"What the hell?" came the muffled tone. As he struggled, she jammed the high heel of her boot down on his foot. There was the muffled sound of a gun going off. Then, while the man was off balance, she placed a well-aimed knee between his legs. He fell to the floor, curled in a fetal position, screaming.

Across the room, Sax was engaged in a battle with both Hollingwood and his enormous bodyguard. The sound of fists hitting flesh was horrible.

Madeline was on her knees, searching through the folds of her coat, desperately searching for the gun Kenyon had dropped. If he recovered his strength before Sax had dispatched his opponents, it would be all over.

She glanced over at Sax just in time to watch his fist connect solidly with the bodyguard's stomach. As the huge opponent toppled to the floor, Madeline had an urge to shout out *timber*.

Returning her attention to finding the gun, she shook the coat; the pistol fell free. Kenyon and Madeline spotted it at the same time. Each dived for the weapon. Madeline reached it first. "Don't even try it," she warned, pointing the gun at Kenyon's chest. Her arm, for some unknown reason, was beginning to shake. She took a deep breath and refused to give in to the unsettling vertigo that was trying to overcome her.

"You wouldn't shoot," Kenyon sneered. "You don't have the guts."

"Oh, no?" She aimed at a spot just to the right of his head and pulled the trigger. Glass shattered from the window she'd shot out, falling around Kenyon's head and shoulders. "You're next," Madeline warned mildly.

Kenyon's arms were over his head, his shoulders hunched, his eyes wide with terror. Deciding that she'd made her point, Maddy looked around just in time to see Hollingwood go flying over the desk with a force and speed that left her dazed. And then Sax was straddling the billionaire crime lord, pounding his fists again and again into the man's face.

"Sax," she cried out, "stop that." She heard the unmistakable crack of a bone breaking; blood began pouring from the man's nose. "Sax," she begged, "you're going to kill him."

"He touched you." Sax didn't turn around. The blows continued. "The bastard touched you."

"But he didn't hurt me." Wanting to go to him, she tried to stand up and discovered that her legs were far from steady. "Please, Sax." Her voice was little more than a whisper. "Please stop. For me."

Before he could answer, the door to the office opened. "I'll take that off your hands, Maddy."

Still on her knees, she looked up into Murphy's smiling freckled face. "You're welcome to it," she breathed with a rush of relief.

"It's about time you guys got here," Sax muttered, scowling at the uniformed men who'd followed Murphy into the room.

"The damn fire marshal had all the streets blocked off. Slowed us up," Murphy said as the other officers quickly dispatched the unholy trio outside into waiting squad cars. "Besides, I don't know why you're so angry. It looks as if you and Maddy had things under control."

"Dumb luck." Sax's scowl darkened further as he bent over Madeline, who had managed to drag herself onto a wooden chair. "You could have been killed, dammit!" His strong hands curved around her shoulders as if to shake her or pull her into his arms; Sax couldn't quite decide.

"Sax." Madeline lifted a trembling hand to his rigid face. "Could you not yell at me, please?"

"I'm not yelling," he yelled.

"Yes, you are. And it's giving me a terrible head-ache." She blinked, fighting off the swirling darkness. "I'm feeling a little funny."

"Shock," Murphy diagnosed.

Concern etched into every grim line of his features, Sax ran his hands down her arms. "Hell." He stared at the red stain on his palms. "Dammit, Maddy, you've gotten yourself shot again!"

"That explains it." Her lips had turned to stone. Was the room tilting or was she?

"I had an ambulance waiting outside, just in case," Murphy said. "I'll go get the paramedics."

"I don't want to waste the time." Sax scooped her into his arms. "I'll take her out to them myself."

"Sax?"

"What now?" His tone was harsh, but she could detect the husky note of caring in it just the same.

"Thank you for trying to help me find Patti." Bright lights swirled on a background of black velvet. She tried to lift her hand to his unsmiling face, but her strength had drained away.

A soft sigh escaped her parted lips as Madeline surrendered to the darkness.

SHE FELT as if she'd awakened in a blizzard. Disoriented, she stared around at the white walls, the white ceiling, the white tile floor. Even the crisp sheet covering her was the color of snow.

And then her puzzled gaze shifted to the man sitting in the too-small vinyl chair beside the bed and she remembered.

"Sax." She managed a wobbly smile. "I'm sorry."

"For what? Saving my life? Or getting shot?"

"For not staying in the apartment like you told me. I almost ruined your plan, didn't I?"

"Things got a little sticky," Sax admitted. "But you didn't ruin anything." He rubbed his hand over his face. His thrusting jaw was darkened by a stubble of beard. "I always knew, from the way the bust went wrong, that there had to be someone working on the inside. I just never would have suspected it was Kenyon. Fortunately Murphy proved quick on the uptake."

He exhaled a deep breath. "I'm sorry I had to say those things to you, Maddy."

She shrugged, then wished she hadn't when the gesture caused a jolt of pain.

"The bullet went right through your shoulder," Sax answered her questioning look. "It was a nice, clean wound, although you lost some blood. The doctor who stitched it up in the emergency room said you'll be good as new in no time."

"Why don't I remember?"

"Because they gave you enough Demerol to knock out a horse."

"Oh." She managed another faint smile. "That's good to know. I don't think I could survive another bout of amnesia."

Her hands were lying at her side on the sheet. He covered one pale hand with his. "Oh, I think you could survive just about anything." He linked their fingers together. "By the way, Hollingwood told us where to find your friend."

"Patti?" Excited, she pushed herself up to a sitting position. "Where is she?"

"In Panama. I know a guy in the DEA, who knows a guy at the CIA, who knows a guy at the State Department. By now she should be at the embassy in Panama City, waiting for an air force jet to bring her back to the States."

"Oh, Sax." Ignoring the pain, Maddy threw her arms around his neck. Her kiss was sweet and warm and broke his heart.

"There's something else," he said once he'd given up possession of those soft lips he knew would taunt his dreams for the rest of his life.

"What?" Her expectant look tugged at something elemental deep inside him.

"You have a visitor."

"Oh, Sax." She dragged her hand through her hair. "I don't think—"

"It's your dad."

"Dad? He's here? In Portland?"

"And driving the nurses crazy," Sax informed her. "Wait here. I'll go get him."

There was something in his eyes. Something he wasn't saying. "Wait." She grabbed his arm. "I'm not going to see you again, am I?"

The answer was written all over his face. It echoed in his eyes. "I don't think that would be a very good idea, Maddy."

"Why not?"

"I told you from the beginning," he reminded her. "I don't have anything to offer you."

All right, if he was going to make her beg, Maddy decided, she'd do it. Begging was far less painful than losing this man she loved. "I wouldn't ask anything you couldn't give, Sax."

"No, you wouldn't." His gaze softened as it swept her face. "Because you're too sweet and too caring. But you deserve a hell of a lot more, Maddy."

"You know, Sax," Maddy said, trying one last time, "we all determine where we want to live. Within our walls. Or outside of them."

The plea shimmering in her eyes almost made him question his resolve. Almost. Giving in to impulse, he lowered his head and brushed his lips against hers. Softly, tenderly. "Have a good life, mermaid. I'll be watching for your byline."

And with one last slow stroke of his hand down the side of her face, he was gone. Out of her hospital room. Out of her life.

THE LOS ANGELES DAY WAS bright and sunny, living up to the city's reputation as the land of perpetual summer. The man who opened the door to Sax's knock was dressed in a blue polo shirt, white tennis shorts and sneakers.

Even if Maddy hadn't told him that her father was a cop, Sax would have recognized the look. Straight-shooting eyes, short hair, lantern jaw. A jaw that was currently jutting his way.

"It's about time you showed up, Carstairs," he growled, glaring at Sax as if he'd like to put a bullet straight into his uninvited visitor's black heart.

"Hello, sir." He forced what he'd hoped was an in-gratiating smile. "It's good to see you again."

"Too bad I can't say the same for you. You're six weeks late."

"I realize that, sir. It's just that I had something I had to do. Some things I had to work out."

"Another woman?"

"No." He met the older man's accusing gaze with a level one of his own. "I didn't want to ask Maddy to be my wife until I felt that I had something of value to offer her."

"And now you do?"

A feeling of déjà vu swept over Sax, and he was suddenly sixteen years old, standing in Margaret Newman's Garden District living room, assuring her physician father that he promised to bring his daughter straight home from the prom. And no speeding.

Sax decided that after the way he'd behaved, he probably deserved to feel uncomfortable. "Yes, sir. I think I do."

Conlan Delaney rubbed his broad jaw. "Maddy seemed to think you had value all by yourself."

"Maddy tends to see only the best in people, sir."

"I know. It's one of her few flaws." He gave Sax another one of those long, probing looks that Sax decided probably worked wonders back in the days when the man had been interrogating prisoners for a living. "I suppose you want to know where she is."

"There's no answer at her apartment in San Diego. Her landlady doesn't know where she is."

Sax could have, of course, found out where Maddy had gone, using his connections, but he decided that this time he was going to do things right. Even if that included asking the formidable Conlan Delaney for his daughter's hand.

"She's not in San Diego at the moment."

Sax nodded. "That was the conclusion I came to."

"You gonna hurt her again?"

"No," Sax said quickly. Firmly. "I'm going to do my best to love her. Sir."

The older man sighed. "So you're going to be my son-in-law." He did not sound thrilled about the idea.

"Yes, sir. If I can talk your daughter into having me, that is."

"Oh, she'll probably say yes," Conlan divulged reluctantly. "The girl's always been smart as a whip, but she does tend to have a dangerous streak of her mother's romantic nature." He shook his head as he considered that for a moment. "If we're going to be related, there's one thing we should probably get out of the way right now." With that, he pulled his arm back and hit Sax square in the jaw with a force that rocked him back on his heels.

"Now I know where Maddy got her right cross," he muttered, rubbing his aching chin.

"I suppose you're going to tell her that I belted you."

It was a challenge. One Sax understood. "I don't see any reason to upset her. And besides," he admitted, "I deserved it."

At that, Conlan threw back his head and laughed, a big, rumbling sound that exploded from his gut. "Come on in and have a beer, son," he said, putting his arm around Sax's shoulders. "We can drink to the upcoming nuptials, and you can meet my bride. Then I'll draw you a map up to the Lake Arrowhead cabin. Maddy's up there, working on a book about that no-account bastard Hollingwood."

One obstacle down, Sax considered as he entered Conlan Delaney's modest but comfortable home.

Only one more to go. He could only hope that along with her mother's romantic nature, Madeline had developed a bit of her father's ability to forgive.

LAKE ARROWHEAD WAS ninety minutes from downtown L.A. in the San Bernadino Mountains. The narrow road leading up to Lake Arrowhead twisted and turned through the wooded hillsides like a tangled fishing line. The trees grew more and more dense as the elevation rose steadily from the desert floor. Stately stands of pines, oaks, cedars, fir and dogwood lined the roadway, casting shadows across the pavement.

A family of deer—a doe and two fawns—were grazing on foliage by the side of the road. Sax slowed the rental car, watched them and felt slightly more relaxed. Then, picking up speed to continue his trek, he felt the knot in his stomach pull tighter again.

He did love her. After he'd left the hospital and returned to the seclusion of his lighthouse, Sax realized that he'd fallen in love with her from the beginning. But he'd been too dense and, although it was damn hard to admit, too terrified at the idea of losing control—of his heart, not to mention his life—to admit it.

But he had fallen. And fallen hard. For her beauty, her mind, her spirit and her courage. Somehow, when he wasn't looking, his mermaid had become the center of his universe, and to continue to ignore that truth was not only stupid, but it was impossible.

Following Conlan Delaney's hand-drawn map, he drove through Lake Arrowhead Village, a mile-high alpine community of fashionable shops and restaurants between Blue Jay Bay and Village Bay. He made a mental note of a beautiful bed-and-breakfast inn at the Saddleback Center, just above the entrance to the village, and considered the fact that it might make a romantic honeymoon location.

"Jumping the gun a bit, aren't you, pal?" he muttered to himself. "The lady hasn't even said she'll have you yet."

But she would, Sax vowed. If he had to use the handcuffs he had stuffed into his duffel bag at the last minute and drag her kicking and screaming to the nearest justice of the peace.

Hoping that it wouldn't come to that, he continued along the lakeside road. But his mind kept drifting to Maddy, and he kept rehearsing his formal proposal again and again, making him miss his turnoff. When he looked around and realized that he had driven nearly the entire circumference of the sparkling blue lake, he swore, then turned around and headed back in the direction from which he'd come.

When he'd left Los Angeles, the sky had been a bright and dazzling blue. As he'd driven up the mountains, a single dark cloud had appeared and seemed to follow him. Never having considered himself a suspicious man, Sax tried not to see the angry gray cloud as a portent.

Until that cloud suddenly opened up, dumping water directly on top of him. A heavy flurry of windblown raindrops pelted against the windshield and streamed down the glass, making vision difficult. His spirits sagging as grimly as the weather, Sax hoped that he'd find Maddy home.

Conlan Delaney's rustic retirement fishing cabin on Bret Harte Road turned out to be a massive A-frame, surrounded by a wide wooden deck, set atop a knoll.

The wide, boat-prow front windows offered a breath-taking view of the lake.

He looked up at the house for a long time, garnering his courage, running through his speech one last time. Then, taking a deep breath that was meant to calm but didn't, he dragged a hand through his dark hair and left the car.

The door lacked a bell. Sax rapped on the carved oak front. Then he waited, rewarded by the sound of footfalls inside the cabin.

"Hello." The attractive young woman who opened the door smiled at him. There was not a sign of recognition on her face or in her eyes. "May I help you?"

Sax glanced at the number on the house, checked Conlan's map one more time and decided that he must have the right place. "I'm looking for Madeline Delaney."

The woman's bright blue eyes narrowed. "Excuse me," she said, closing the door a bit, "do I know you?"

"Sorry." Sax managed a nervous grin that was more grimace than proper smile. "My name is Saxon Carstairs. I'm a friend of Maddy's."

"Saxon Carstairs!" The woman's face bloomed into a smile that made him forget all about the icy raindrops pelting over his head and shoulders. "Well, why didn't you say that right away?" She flung the door open. "Come on in before you catch your death of cold," she invited. "Maddy's working, but I'll go get her. Right after I thank you for rescuing me."

Just as Sax realized that this must be the missing Patti, the blonde threw her arms around his neck and pressed her lips against his.

"Excuse me," a calm, familiar voice broke into the exuberant kiss. "Am I interrupting something?"

Madeline was standing in the doorway, leaning against the doorframe, her arms folded across the front of a bright red sweatshirt emblazoned with loons. He saw none of the pain or desolation or even the anger he'd expected to view in her eyes. Her gaze was level, smooth and frighteningly emotionless.

"I was just thanking Sax for being such a heroic white knight," Patti said with an unembarrassed smile.

Wishing that an earthquake would suddenly rip through these mountains and swallow him up whole, Sax gingerly plucked Patti's arms from around his neck. "Hello, Maddy."

"Hello, Sax." Her noncommittal tone offered not an iota of welcome. But neither was it laced with censure. Sax grasped onto that last thought like a man adrift in a stormy sea grabbing hold of a piece of driftwood.

Neither of them said a word. They both stood there, no more than eight feet apart, divided by a chasm that suddenly seemed as deep and wide as the Grand Canyon.

"Well, I've got some shopping to do in the village," Patti said, her smiling gaze going from Madeline to Sax, then Madeline again. "And then I think I'll have dinner and a show. You two have a nice chat." She left the room, humming happily beneath her breath.

Maddy was the first to break the silence. "You're late."

"That's the same thing your father said."

"My father has a knack for being right. He's also very protective, just like some other man I thought I used to know."

"I found that out."

Her steady gaze moved from his eyes to his swollen jaw. "Did he do that?"

Sax merely shrugged.

"I suppose I should apologize," Maddy said. "But I don't think I will. Since he only did what I've been wanting to do for weeks."

Sax decided it was time to back away from the subject of his apparent abandonment. "I read your series of articles on Hollingwood," he said. "The *Oregonian* picked them up from the *Union*."

It was Maddy's turn to shrug. "So did a lot of other papers."

"I heard rumors that you were going to be nominated for a Pulitzer."

Another brief shrug. "Journalism runs on rumors. I'll believe it when I see it."

Another strained silence settled over them. "Your father said you were working on a book," Sax said.

"That's right. I was approached by a surprising amount of publishers after the story broke. I hadn't really considered writing books, but I'm finding that I'm enjoying the work a lot."

The suspense, and her continuing distance, was making him crazy. Sax wanted to go to her, to drag her into his arms, to cover her lovely, impassive face with kisses and beg her to forgive him for not being the man she'd hoped that he could be.

"I seem to remember you telling me that you never lied," he said instead.

"I don't."

"But you said you'd never thought about writing books. That's not exactly true, is it?"

He watched the memory flood into her eyes. Her cheeks flushed the color of the cranberries growing in the bogs outside of Satan's Cove. Her lip began to tremble, the first display of emotion he'd seen since she'd appeared in the doorway and caught him in a compromising position with her best friend.

"That seems like another lifetime ago," she murmured.

"Sometimes it seems like a lifetime ago," Sax agreed. "Other times it seems like yesterday. I brought you something." Wordlessly he crossed the room and held out the package.

Giving him a quizzical look, she loosened the brown-paper wrapping. "Oh, Sax," she breathed. She sank down onto a nearby chintz-covered chair and began leafing through the photographs. "It's our lighthouse. And our jetty." She looked up at him, her eyes shining like those of a woman who'd just been handed a treasure trove of precious gems. "Thank you. I'll treasure these always."

He took heart in the fact that she'd said *our* lighthouse. And *our* jetty. "There's just one problem," he said with feigned casualness, even as his heart was pounding against his ribs.

Her gaze had returned to the photographs. She ran her fingers over one particular photograph of whales breaching, and a faint smile of remembrance curved her lips. "What problem? They're perfect."

"Ellen already has a publisher interested," he divulged. "But it's not much of a book without a text." That captured her immediate attention. She looked up at him, the hope he was feeling in his own heart shimmering beautifully in her eyes. "I was hoping that perhaps, if I was lucky, I could find a Pulitzer Prize–caliber writer to collaborate with me," he said.

Her brow furrowed. "Are you asking me to write the text for your book?"

"It was your suggestion," he reminded her. "And not just this book. I figure I've got a lot more photographs in me. And they'll all need text."

She thought about that for a moment. "I'd want a contract."

"Absolutely. And I promise, there'll be plenty of time for you to work on your book."

Madeline nodded. "When would you want to get started?"

"Right away. If that's all right with you."

"It's fine." She glanced through the photographs again. "I suppose you could just leave these with me, and—"

"I was hoping that you'd come with me," Sax cut in. "So we could work on the book together."

"You want me to live with you?"

"Yes, but—"

It was Madeline's turn to interrupt him. "Where?"

Details. The woman definitely wasn't going to make it easy on him. But Sax wondered why she should. After all, he couldn't deny that he'd treated her worse than he used to treat the lowlifes he'd dragged in for booking.

"San Diego. Portland. Hell, wherever you want."

Pleased that Sax was willing to rejoin the world, Madeline pretended to think the matter over. "I love your apartment in Portland," she said at length. "But there's something about the lighthouse that's special, too."

"We could always keep it as a getaway place." He wanted to go to her, to drag her into his arms, to make love to her. But he remained where he was, waiting for her to make the first move.

"Oh, I like that idea," Madeline said with a smile. "Well, it certainly seems as if you've given the matter a great deal of thought."

"I have."

She nodded. She wanted to go to him. To fling herself into his arms. But she didn't dare touch him, because if she did, all her resolve would dissolve.

He had come to her, as she'd known all along he would. But there was something else she wanted. Madeline knew that she could demand the words from him and probably get her way. But she needed the admission to come from his heart.

The silence hovered between them, as thick as morning fog.

"There's something else," Sax ventured. Never in all his years walking a beat in Portland's dangerous waterfront district, or his later years spent as a vice cop, had he ever been this nervous.

"Oh?"

He raked his fingers through his hair, took another deep breath and crossed the space between them to stand in front of her. "I love you, Madeline Anne Delaney. And I want to marry you. And have children with you, if you're willing, and grow old walking hand in hand along the beach, watching the sunsets. I want a lifetime of sunsets with you, mermaid."

A dazzling smile bloomed on her face; her eyes were wet and brilliant. "I was beginning to think you'd never ask."

"Is that a yes?"

"I love you, Sax. I've loved you for ages. Of course I'll marry you."

Sax drew her into his arms with a deep sigh of relief. "God, I've missed you." He kissed her long and hard. "Do you have any idea how difficult these last weeks have been?"

"They haven't exactly been a picnic for me, either," she assured him against his lips. "So don't you think we should be making up for lost time?"

"I knew I was marrying an extremely intelligent woman." Sax scooped her effortlessly into his arms. "Which way to the bedroom?"

Twining her arms around his neck, Madeline laughed and proceeded to give him directions.

Earth, Wind, Fire, Water
**The four elements—but nothing is
more elemental than passion.**

Join us for

Four sizzling action-packed romances in the tradition of
Romancing the Stone and *The African Queen*. Starting January
1994, one book each month is a sexy, romantic adventure
focusing on the quest for passion...set against the essential
elements of earth, wind, fire and water.

On sale in January
To melt away the winter blues, there's *Body Heat* by
Elise Title, bestselling author of the Fortune Boys series.

To win the hot role of an arson investigator, movie star
Rebecca Fox knew she had to experience the heat of a
real-life investigation. So she sought out the best one in
the business—Zach Chapin. Soon Rebecca and Zack were
generating more heat than the torch they were tailing.

The quest continues...
Coming in February... *Wild Like The Wind* by Janice Kaiser.

*Passion's Quest—four fantastic adventures,
four fantastic love stories*

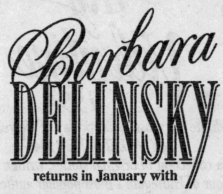

My Valentine 1994

Celebrate the most romantic day of the year with
MY VALENTINE 1994
a collection of original stories, written by
four of Harlequin's most popular authors...

**MARGOT DALTON
MURIEL JENSEN
MARISA CARROLL
KAREN YOUNG**

Available in February, wherever
Harlequin Books are sold.

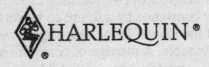

HARLEQUIN ®

VAL94

When the only time you have for yourself is…

STOLEN *moments* ™

Christmas is such a busy time—with shopping, decorating, writing
cards, trimming trees, wrapping gifts….

When you do have a few *stolen moments* to call your own, treat yourself
to a brand-new *short* novel. Relax with one of our Stocking Stuffers—
or with all six!

Each STOLEN MOMENTS title
is a complete and original contemporary romance that's the perfect
length for the busy woman of the nineties! Especially at Christmas…

And they make perfect **stocking stuffers**, too! (For your mother,
grandmother, daughters, friends, co-workers, neighbors, aunts,
cousins—all the other women in your life!)

Look for the STOLEN MOMENTS display in December

STOCKING STUFFERS:

HIS MISTRESS Carrie Alexander
DANIEL'S DECEPTION Marie DeWitt
SNOW ANGEL Isolde Evans
THE FAMILY MAN Danielle Kelly
THE LONE WOLF Ellen Rogers
MONTANA CHRISTMAS Lynn Russell

HSM2

 W❂RLDWIDE LIBRARY ®

HARLEQUIN®
Temptation

If you missed any Lovers & Legends titles,
here's your chance to order them:

Harlequin Temptation®—Lovers & Legends

#425	THE PERFECT HUSBAND by Kristine Rolofson	$2.99 ☐
#433	THE MISSING HEIR by Leandra Logan	$2.99 ☐
#437	DR. HUNK by Glenda Sanders	$2.99 ☐
#441	THE VIRGIN AND THE UNICORN by Kelly Street	$2.99 ☐
#445	WHEN IT'S RIGHT by Gina Wilkins	$2.99 ☐
#449	SECOND SIGHT by Lynn Michaels	$2.99 ☐
#453	THE PRINCE AND THE SHOWGIRL by JoAnn Ross	$2.99 ☐
#457	YOU GO TO MY HEAD by Bobby Hutchinson	$2.99 ☐
#461	NIGHT WATCH by Carla Neggers	$2.99 ☐
#465	NAUGHTY TALK by Tiffany White	$2.99 ☐
#469	I'LL BE SEEING YOU by Kristine Rolofson	$2.99 ☐

(limited quantities available on certain titles)

TOTAL AMOUNT	$	
POSTAGE & HANDLING	$	
($1.00 for one book, 50¢ for each additional)		
APPLICABLE TAXES*	$	
TOTAL PAYABLE	$	_____
(check or money order—please do not send cash)		_____

To order, complete this form and send it, along with a check or money order for the total above, payable to Harlequin Books, to: *In the U.S.*: 3010 Walden Avenue, P.O. Box 9047, Buffalo, NY 14269-9047; *In Canada*: P.O. Box 613, Fort Erie, Ontario, L2A 5X3.

Name: _____

Address: _____City: _____

State/Prov.: _____Zip/Postal Code: _____

*New York residents remit applicable sales taxes.
Canadian residents remit applicable GST and provincial taxes.

LLF